THE KREUTZER SONATA

by Leo Tolstoy

adapted by JOSEPH COWLEY

iUniverse, Inc.
Bloomington

The Kreutzer Sonata by Leo Tolstoy
Adapted by Joseph Cowley

iUniverse books may be ordered through booksellers or by contacting:

iUniverse
1663 Liberty Drive
Bloomington, IN 47403
www.iuniverse.com
1-800-Authors (1-800-288-4677)

ISBN: 978-1-4759-1733-8 (sc)
ISBN: 978-1-4759-1732-1 (e)

Printed in the United States of America

iUniverse rev. date: 5/9/2012

This work meets the requirements for level 4 of the Ladder series for ESL students. Photo of Tolstoy courtesy of Wickipedia.

For Bernice Friedson
for her help and
encouragement.
JGC

TABLE OF CONTENTS

CHAPTER I

Passengers left and entered our car at every stop the train made. Three persons, however, stayed in the car, bound, like myself, for the furthest station. One was a lady, neither young nor pretty, who was smoking cigarettes. She had a thin face, and was wearing a cap on her head and a man's coat. Her companion was a gentleman of about forty, his travel bags arranged in an orderly manner, who liked to talk. The third was a gentleman who kept himself apart.

This latter gentleman was short in height, and one couldn't be certain about his age. He seemed anxious, with bright, pale eyes that went rapidly from one object to another. During almost all the journey thus far he had talked to none of his fellow passengers, as if avoiding all company. When spoken to, he answered briefly and looked out the car window as if to avoid further conversation.

Yet, it seemed to me, he was lonely. He seemed to know I understood this, and when our eyes met, as happened frequently, since we were sitting opposite each other, he turned away his head to avoid conversation with me as much as with the others.

As it was getting dark, during a stop at a large station, the gentleman with the fine bags – a lawyer, as I since learned – got out with his companion to drink some tea at the restaurant. While they were gone, several new passengers entered the car, among them a tall old man, shaven and wrinkled, a merchant by the looks of him, wearing a large fur-lined coat and a big cap.

He sat down opposite the empty seats of the lawyer and his companion, and immediately started talking to a young man who

1

appeared to be an employee in some business house. He had also just gotten on the train.

The young man said that the seat opposite was occupied, and the old man answered that he was getting out at the first station. Thus their conversation started.

I was sitting not far from these two passengers, and, as the train was not in motion, I caught bits of their conversation when others were not talking. They talked first of the prices of goods and the condition of business.

Next they mentioned a person whom they both knew, then plunged into a discussion of the fair at Nijni Novgorod, from which they must have both just come.

The young man made much of knowing people who were leading a gay life there, but the old man did not allow him to continue, and began describing what had gone on the previous year at Kounavino.

He seemed proud of these memories, and, probably thinking this would take nothing from the seriousness his face and manners expressed, he told with pride how, when drunk, he fired such a broad-side that he could describe it only in the other's ear.

The young man laughed noisily. The old man laughed, too, showing two long yellow teeth. Their conversation did not interest me, and I left the car to stretch my legs. At the door I met the lawyer and his lady.

"You have no more time," the lawyer said to me. "The second bell is about to ring."

Indeed I had scarcely reached the rear of the train when the bell sounded. I returned to the car. As I entered, the lawyer was talking with his companion in an excited fashion. The merchant, sitting opposite them, was quiet.

"And then she declared to her husband," said the lawyer with a smile as I passed by them, "that she neither could nor would live with him, because..."

He continued talking, but I did not hear the rest of the sentence. My attention was divided by the passing of the conductor and the entrance of a new passenger.

When silence returned, I again heard the lawyer's voice. The conversation had passed from a special case to more general things.

"Afterwards comes unhappiness, money problems, arguments between the two parties, and the couple separate. In the good old days that seldom happened. Is it not so?" asked the lawyer of the merchant and young man, evidently trying to drag them into the conversation.

Just then the train started, and the old man, without answering, took off his cap, and crossed himself three times while quietly saying a prayer. When he finished, he pulled his cap far down on his head, and said:

"Yes, sir, that happened in former times also, but not as often. In the present day it is bound to happen more frequently. People have become too learned."

The lawyer made some reply to the old man, but the train, increasing its speed, made such a noise on the rails that I could no longer hear clearly.

As I was interested in what the old man was saying, I drew nearer. My neighbor, the anxious gentleman, must have been interested also, for, without changing his seat, he leaned forward to hear better.

"But what harm is there in education?" asked the lady, with a smile that was hardly noticeable. "Would it be better to marry as in the old days, when the man and woman did not even see each other before marriage?

"Women did not know whether they would love or be loved, and they were married to the first comer, and suffered all their lives. You think it was better so?" she went on, speaking to the lawyer and myself, not to the old man.

"People have become too learned," repeated the old man, not answering her question.

"I should be curious to know how you explain the connection between education and difficulties when one is married," said the lawyer with a slight smile.

The merchant wanted to answer, but the lady interrupted him.

"No, those days are past."

The lawyer cut her short: "Let him express his thought."

"Because there is no more fear," said the old man.

"But how will you marry people who do not love each other?" said the lady. "Only animals can be coupled at the will of someone else. People have desires, likings," she said, glancing at the lawyer, at me, and even at the young man, who was standing up and leaning on the back of a seat, listening to the conversation with a smile.

"You are wrong to say that, Madam," said the old man. "The animals are beasts, but man has received the law."

"But, nevertheless, how is one to live with a man when there is no love?" said the lady, excited by the general sympathy and attention she was receiving.

"Formerly no such differences were made," said the old man gravely. "Only now have they become a part of our habits. As soon as the least thing happens, the wife says: 'I free you. I am going to leave your house. There,' she says, 'are your shirts and drawers. I am going off with Vanka. His hair has more curls than yours.' And yet the first rule for the wife should be fear."

The young man looked at the lawyer, the lady, and myself, hiding a smile, and ready to agree or not to agree with the merchant, according to the attitude of the others.

"What fear?" said the lady.

"This fear – the wife must fear her husband; that is what fear."

"Oh, that, my little father, that is ended."

"No, Madam, that cannot end. As she, Eve, the woman, was taken from man's ribs, so she will remain to the end of the world," said the old man, shaking his head so confidently that the young man, deciding the victory was on his side, burst into a loud laugh.

"Yes, you men think so," replied the lady, and turning toward us said, "You have given yourself liberty. As for the woman, you wish to keep her as a slave in the home. To you, everything is permitted. Is it not so?"

"Oh, that's another matter," said the merchant.

"Then, according to you, to man everything is permitted?"

"No one gives him this permission. Only, if the man acts badly outside, the family is not increased by what he does. But the woman, the wife, is a weaker vessel."

His tone of authority seemed to put his listeners down. Even the lady felt crushed. But she did not give in.

"Yes, but you will admit, I think, that a woman is a human being, and has feelings like her husband. What should she do if she does not love her husband?"

"If she does not love him!" repeated the old man angrily; "Why, she will be made to love him."

This argument pleased the young man, and he made sounds of agreement.

"Oh, no, she will not be forced," said the lady. "Where there is no love, one cannot be obliged to love."

"And if the wife wrongs her husband, what is to be done?" said the lawyer.

"That should not happen," said the old man. "He must have his eyes about him."

"And if it does happen, all the same? You will admit that it does happen?"

"It happens among the upper classes, not among us," answered the old man. "If any husband is found who is such a fool as not to rule his wife, he will not have been robbed by her. But in any case there should be no scenes. Love or not, but do not destroy the peace of the household. Every husband can govern his wife. He has the necessary power. It is only the fool who cannot do so."

Everybody was silent. The young man moved forward and, not wishing to fall behind the others in the conversation, said, with his ever present smile:

"Yes, in the house of our employer a scene has risen, and it is very difficult to view the matter clearly. The wife loved to enjoy herself, and began to go wrong.

"He is an able and serious man. First, she fooled around with the book-keeper. The husband tried to bring her back to reason through kindness. She did not change her conduct. She started doing all sorts of bad things.

"She began to steal his money. He beat her, but she grew worse. She slept with one who does not believe in God, with a Jew (saving your permission), with one after the other. What could the employer do? He dropped her, and now lives alone. As for her, she is dragging bottom."

"He is a fool," said the old man. "If from the first he had not allowed her to go on in her own fashion, and had kept a firm hand upon her, she would be living honestly. Liberty must be taken from the woman from the very beginning. "As the saying goes: Do not trust your horse on the road. Do not trust your wife at home."

At that moment the conductor passed, asking for the tickets for the next station. The old man gave up his.

"Yes, the female sex must be ruled, else all will be lost," he added.

"And you yourselves, at Kounavino, did you not lead a gay life with the pretty girls?" asked the lawyer with a smile.

"Oh, that's another matter," said the merchant gravely. "Good-by," he added, rising. He wrapped himself in his coat, lifted his cap, and, taking his bag, left the car.

CHAPTER II

Hardly had the old man gone when a general conversation began.

"There's a little Old Testament father for you," said the young man.

"He is a Domostrov,"*" said the lady. "What savage ideas about women and marriage!"

"Yes," said the lawyer, "we are still a long way from the European ideas upon marriage. First, the rights of women, then freedom to marry whom we choose, then divorce, are questions not yet solved."

"The thing such people do not understand," said the lady, 'is that to be married is real when it is made holy by love."

The young listened and smiled with the air of one who liked to store in his memory all the interesting conversation he hears in order to make use of it afterward.

"But what is this love that makes being married holy?" said suddenly the voice of the quiet, anxious gentleman who, unnoticed, had approached and was standing with his hand on the seat, quite excited.

His face was red, a blood vessel in his forehead was swollen, and the muscles of his cheeks shook.

"What is this love that makes marriage holy?" he repeated.

"What love?" answered the lady. "The ordinary love of husband and wife."

"And how, then, can ordinary love make being married holy?" continued the gentleman, still excited, and with an air of not being

---

* The Domostrovs was a religious group existing at the time of Ivan the Terrible.

pleased by her answer. He seemed to wish to say something that might not be agreeable to the lady. She felt it, and began to grow excited, too.

"How? Why, very simply," said she.

The gentleman seized the word as it left her lips.

"No, not simply."

"Madam says," put in the lawyer, indicating his companion, "that being married should be first the result of a liking, of a love, if you will, and that, when love exists, and in that case only, being married represents something holy. But to marry without a natural liking and respect, without love, has in it nothing that is morally acceptable.

"Is not that what you wished to say?" he asked, turning to the lady.

The lady, with a nod of her head, expressed her agreement.

"Then…" continued the lawyer.

But the anxious gentleman, excited and scarcely able to contain himself, without allowing the lawyer to finish asked: "Yes, sir. But what are we to understand by this love that alone makes being married holy?"

"Everybody knows what love is," said the lady.

"But I don't, and I should like to know how you define it."

"How? It is very simple," said the lady.

After a few moments of thought, she said: "Love is a preference for one man or one woman above all others."

"A preference for how long? For a month, two days, or half an hour?" said the gentleman, with some heat.

"No, permit me," said the lawyer, "I don't think you are talking of the same thing."

"Yes, I am talking absolutely of the same thing. Of the preference for one man or one woman above all others. But I ask: a preference for how long?"

"For how long? For a long time, for a life-time sometimes."

"But that happens only in novels. In life, never. In life this preference for one above all others lasts, in rare cases, several years, more often several months, or even weeks, days, hours."

"Oh, sir. Oh, no, no, permit me," said all three of us at the same time.

The young man made a noise showing he didn't agree.

"Yes, I know," the gentleman said, shouting louder than all of us. "You are talking of what is believed to exist, and I am talking of what *is*. Every man feels what you call love toward each pretty woman he sees, and very little toward his wife. That is the origin of the saying – and it is a true one – 'Another's wife is a white swan, and ours is an ugly duck.'"

"Ah, but what you say is terrible! There certainly exists among human beings this feeling called love, which lasts, not for months and years, but for life."

"No, that does not exist. Even if it should be admitted that Menelaus had preferred Helen all his life, Helen would have preferred Paris; and so it has been, is, and will be forever. And it cannot be otherwise, just as it cannot happen that, in a load of chick-peas, two peas marked with a special sign should fall side by side.

"Further, this is not only not likely, but it is certain that a feeling of having had enough will come to Helen or to Menelaus. The whole difference is that to one it comes sooner, to the other later.

"It is only in novels that it is written that 'they loved each other all their lives.' And none but children can believe it. To talk of loving a man or woman for life is like saying that a candle can burn forever."

"But you are talking of physical love. Do you not admit there is a love based upon an agreement of ideals, on a holy unity?"

"Why not? But in that case it is not necessary to make children together (excuse my language). The point is that this agreement of ideals is not met among old people, but among young and pretty persons," said he.

He began to laugh in a way that was not agreeable.

"Yes," he went on, "I say that love, real love, does not make being married holy, as we are in the habit of believing, but that, on the contrary, it ruins it."

"Permit me," said the lawyer. "The facts do not match your words. We see that to be married exists, that all humanity – at least the larger portion – lives as man and wife, and that many husbands and wives honestly end a long life together."

The anxious gentleman smiled ill-naturedly.

"And what then? You say that being married is based upon love, and when I give voice to a doubt as to the existence of any other love than physical love, you prove to me the existence of love by being married. But in our day to be married is only fighting and lies."

"No, pardon me," said the lawyer. "I say only that to be married has existed and does exist."

"But how and why does being married exist? That state has existed, and does exist, for people who have seen, and do see, in being married something holy, something that is binding before God. For such people being married exists, but to us it is only lies and fighting.

"We feel it, and, to clear ourselves, we speak of free love. But free love is only a call back to a life without principles between man and woman (excuse me, he said to the lady), the chance sin of certain raskolniks.** The old foundation is broken; we must build a new one, but we must not build it on sin."

He grew so excited that all became silent, looking at him.

"And yet this state of change is terrible. People feel that sin is not permitted. It is necessary in some way or other to control the relations between a man and a woman. But does there exist no other basis than the old one, in which nobody longer believes?

"People marry in the old fashion, without believing in what they do, and the result is lies, and fighting. When it is lies alone, it is easily endured. The husband and wife simply put up a false front to the world by claiming to live for each other alone. If they really are having relations with others, it is bad, but acceptable.

"But when, as often happens, the husband and the wife have taken upon themselves the duty to live together all their lives (they themselves do not know why), and from the second month have already a desire to separate, but continue to live together just the same, then comes that existence in hell, in which they turn to drink, fire guns to kill each other, or poison each other."

All were silent, but we felt ill at ease.

"Yes, these things happen in married life. For instance, there is the Posdnicheff affair," said the lawyer, wishing to stop the conversation on this too exciting and not comfortable ground. "Have you read how he killed his wife through passion?"

** *Raskolnikov is a character in Dostoevsky's* Crime and Punishment.

The lady said that she had not read it. The anxious gentleman said nothing, and changed color.

"I see that you have guessed who I am," said he suddenly, after a pause.

"No, I have not had that pleasure."

"It is no great pleasure. I am Posdnicheff."

New silence. He turned red, then pale again.

"What matters it, however?" said he. "Excuse me, I do not wish to make you ill at ease."

And he returned to his old seat.

CHAPTER III

I retuned to my seat, also. The lawyer and the lady were whispering together. I sat beside Posdnicheff and kept silent. I wanted to talk to him, but did not know how to begin.

Thus an hour passed until we reached the next station. There the lawyer and the lady went out, as well as the young man. We were left alone, Posdnicheff and I.

"They say it and they lie, or they do not understand," said Posdnicheff.

"Of what are you talking?"

"Why, still the same thing."

He leaned his elbows on his knees and pressed his hands against his temples.

"Love, being married, family – all lies, lies, lies."

He rose, lowered the lamp-shade, lay down with his elbows on the seat, and closed his eyes.

He remained thus for a minute.

"Does it not make you ill at ease to remain with me, now that you know who I am?"

"Oh, no."

"You have no desire to sleep?"

"Not at all."

"Then do you want me to tell you the story of my life?"

Just then the conductor passed. Posdnicheff gave him an ill-natured look, and did not begin again until he had gone. Then during all the rest of the story he did not stop once. Even new passengers entering the car did not stop him.

His face while he talked changed several times, so completely that it bore little likeness to itself as it had appeared just before. His eyes, his mouth, even his hair, all were new.

Each time it was a beautiful and touching the way these changes were produced suddenly in the shadows. For five minutes it was the same face, but could not be compared to that of five minutes before.

And then, I know not how, it changed again, and became a face I did not recognize.

CHAPTER IV

"Well, I am going then to tell you about my life, and my whole terrible history – yes, terrible. And the story itself is more terrible than the outcome."

He was silent for a moment, passed his hands over his eyes, and began: "To be understood clearly, the whole must be told from the beginning. You have to understand how and why I married, and what I was before I was married.

"First, I will tell you who I am. The son of a rich gentleman of the country, a senior officer of the upper class, I was a University pupil, a graduate of the law school. I married when I was thirty. But before telling you of my married life, I must tell you how I lived before that, and what ideas I had of married life.

"I led the life of so many other so-called respectable people – that is, I lived in sin. And like most people, while leading the life of a sinner I believed I was a man of the highest morals.

"The idea I had of my morality came from the fact that in my family there was no knowledge of those sins so common in the surroundings of land-owners, and also from the fact that my father and my mother were honest with each other.

"As a result, I had from childhood a dream of a high and perfect married life. My wife was to be perfection itself, our love for each other was to be beyond compare, the purity of our married life without anything to spoil it. I thought thus, and all the time I marveled at how noble all the things I planned were.

"At the same time, I passed ten years of my adult life without being in a hurry to marry, living what I called the well-regulated and reasonable life of a bachelor. I was proud of it before my friends, and before all men of my age who gave themselves to all sorts of activities.

"I did not lead women into sin, I had no tastes that were not natural, and I did not make living a life of sin the principal object of my life. But I found pleasure within the limits of society's rules, and innocently believed myself a deeply moral being.

"The women with whom I had relations did not belong to me alone, and I asked of them nothing but the pleasure of the moment. In all this I saw nothing out of the ordinary. And from the fact that I did not engage my heart, but paid in cash, I supposed that I was honest.

"I avoided those women who, by tying themselves to me, or presenting me with a child, could bind my future. Moreover, perhaps there may have been children or ties; but I so arranged matters that I could not become aware of them.

"And living thus, I considered myself a perfectly honest man. I did not understand that sin is not simply a physical act. Physical acts, I thought, do not yet mean one has sinned. Now I know that real sin consists in being free from the moral bonds toward a woman with whom one enters into physical relations.

"At the time, I regarded THIS FREEDOM as a good thing. I remember that I once suffered greatly for having forgotten to pay a woman who probably had given herself to me through love. I only became at peace again when, having sent her the money, I had thus shown her that I did not consider myself as in any way bound to her.

"Oh, do not shake your head as if you were in agreement with me (he cried suddenly). I know these tricks. All of you, and you especially if you are not a rare exception, have the same ideas I had then.

"If you are in agreement with me, it is now only. Formerly you did not think so. No more did I; and, if I had been told what I have just told you, that which has happened would not have happened.

"However, it is all the same. Excuse me (he continued): the truth is that it is terrible, terrible, these errors and sins in which we live, face to face with the real question of the rights of woman…"

"What do you mean by the 'real' question of the rights of woman?"

"The question of the nature of this special being, organized otherwise than man, and how this being and man ought to view the wife. . . ."

Chapter V

"Yes: for ten years I lived the most terrible existence, while dreaming of the noblest love, and even in the name of that love. Yes, I want to tell you how I killed my wife, and for that I must tell you how I ruined myself.

"I killed her before I knew her. I killed THE wife when I first tasted physical joys without love, and then it was that I killed MY wife. Yes, sir: it is only after having suffered, after having put myself through much pain, that I have come to understand the root of things, that I have come to understand my crimes. Thus you will see where and how began the life that has led me to this pass.

"It is necessary to go back to my sixteenth year, when I was still at school, and my older brother a first-year student. I had not yet known women but, like all the children of our society, I was already no longer innocent.

"I was guilt ridden, as you were, I am sure, and as are ninety-nine one-hundredths of our boys. I lived in a terrible fear, I prayed to God, and I humbled myself.

"I was already a sinner in thoughts, but the last steps remained to be taken. I could still escape, when a friend of my brother, a very gay student, one of those who are called good fellows – that is, the greatest of evil doers – and who had taught us to drink and play cards, took advantage of a night when we were all drunk to drag us THERE.

"We started. My brother, as innocent as I, fell that night, and I, a mere lad of sixteen, dirtied myself and helped to dirty a sister-woman, without understanding what I did. Never had I heard from those older than myself that what I did was bad. It is true that there are the ten commands of the Bible; but those are made only to be repeated before the priests when being examined.

"Thus, from those who were older, whose opinion I cared for, I never heard that this was bad and not to be done. On the other hand, I had heard people whom I respected say that it was good. I had heard that my struggles and my sufferings would be eased after this act.

"I had heard it and read it. I had heard from those older than myself that it was excellent for the health, and my friends have always seemed to believe that it contained I know not what value and good. So nothing bad is seen in it but what is praised.

"As for the danger of disease, it is a known danger. But does not the government guard against it? And even science helps us to sin."

"How so, science?" I asked.

"Why, the doctors, the leaders of science. Who make it possible for young people to sin by laying down rules for avoiding disease? Who permits women to sin by teaching them ways by which not to have children?

"If only a hundredth of the efforts spent in curing diseases were spent in curing sin, disease would long ago have ceased to exist. Whereas, now, all efforts are employed, not in getting rid of sin, but in favoring it, by assuring us no harm will come as a result.

"Besides, it is not a question of just that. It is a question of this terrible thing that has happened to me, as it happens to nine-tenths, if not more, not only of the men of our society, but of all societies, even the lower classes – this terrible thing, that I had fallen, and not because I was subjected to the natural desire of a certain woman.

"No, no woman desired me. I fell because the surroundings in which I found myself saw in this awful act only something useful to the health; because others saw in it simply a natural pleasure, not only excused, but even harmless in a young man.

"I did not understand that it was a fall, and I began to give myself to those pleasures (partly from desire and partly from need) which I was led to believe were part of being my age, just as I had begun to drink and smoke.

"And yet there was in this first fall something odd and touching. I remember that straight-way I was filled with such a deep sadness that I had a desire to weep, to weep over the loss forever of my relations with women.

"Yes, my relations with women were lost forever. Pure relations with women, from that time forward, I could no longer have. I had become what is called a lost man. And to be lost is a physical condition like the condition of a victim of a drug habit, a drunk, or a smoker.

"Just as the victim of a drug habit, the drunk and the smoker, are no longer normal men, so the man who has known several women for his pleasure is no longer normal. He will never be normal again. He is one who lives for his physical pleasure. Just as the drunk and the drug user may be recognized by their face and manner, so we may recognize one who lives only for his physical pleasures.

"He may struggle to overcome it, but never more will he enjoy simple and pure relations toward women. By his way of glancing at a young woman one may at once recognize one who has only the satisfaction of his physical pleasures in mind. And I became such a person, and have remained one."

CHAPTER VI

"When I hear people talk of the golden youth of the officers, of the Parisians, and all these gentlemen and myself living wild lives at the age of thirty, who have on our guilty minds hundreds of crimes toward women, and who, when we enter a living room or a ball-room, washed and shaven, with very white shirts, in dress coats or in uniform, as signs of purity, oh, the self hate!

"There will surely come a time when all these lives and all these doings will be laid open! But, nevertheless, so I lived, until the age of thirty, without giving up for a minute my aim of one day being married, and building an ideal married life. And with this in view, I watched all young girls who might suit me.

"I was buried in the basest of behavior, and at the same time I looked for young women of virtue, whose purity was worthy of me! Many of them I turned away from: they did not seem to me pure enough!

"Finally I found one I considered on a level worthy of me, someone who was once very rich and had since been ruined. To tell the truth, without saying what is false, they came after me and finally caught me. The mother (the father was away) laid all sorts of traps, and one of these, a trip in a boat, decided my future.

"I made up my mind at the end of that trip one night, by the light of the moon on our way home. While sitting beside her. I admired her body, whose charming shape could be seen through her thin clothing, and her hair, and I suddenly concluded that THIS WAS SHE.

"It seemed to me on that beautiful evening that she understood all that I thought and felt, and I thought and felt the most moving things.

But, really, it was only the thin clothing that was so becoming to her, and her curled hair, and also the fact that I had spent the day beside her, and that I desired a closer relation.

"I returned home full of joy, and I told myself that she realized the highest perfection, and that for that reason she was worthy to be my wife, and the next day I asked her marry me. No, say what you will, we live in such a deep falsity, that, unless some event strikes us a blow on the head, as in my case, we cannot wake up.

"What awfulness!

"Out of the thousands of men who marry, not only among us, but also among the people, scarcely will you find a single one who has not been married before at least ten times.

"It is true that there now exist, at least so I have heard, pure young people who feel and know that this is not a joke, but a serious matter. May God come to their aid! But in my time there was not to be found one such in a thousand.

"All know it, and make believe not to know it. In all the novels are described down to the smallest details the feelings of the characters, the lakes and bushes around which they walk. But when it comes to describing their GREAT love, not a word is breathed of what HE, the interesting character, has done before, not a word about his frequenting houses of ill fame, or his association with maids, cooks, and the wives of others.

"And if anything is said of these things, such IMPROPER novels are not allowed in the hands of young girls. All men have the air of believing, in the presence of young women, that these evil pleasures, in which EVERYBODY takes part, do not exist, or exist only to a very small degree. They make believe it doesn't exist so carefully that they succeed in not believing it themselves.

"As for the poor young girls, they believe it quite seriously, just as my poor wife believed it.

"I remember that, being already engaged, I showed her my private 'notes,' from which she could learn more or less of my past, and especially my last affair, which she might perhaps have discovered through the talk of some third party. It was for this last reason, for that matter, that I felt it necessary to give her these personal notes.

"I can still see her fear, her despair, her lack of believing, when she had learned and understood it. She was on the point of breaking our being engaged. What a lucky thing it would have been for both of us!"

Posdnicheff was silent for a moment, and then began again: "After all, no! It is better that things happened as they did, better!" he cried. "It was a good thing for me. Besides, it makes no difference.

"I was saying that in these cases it is the poor young girls who are fooled. As for the mothers, the mothers especially, informed by their husbands, they know all, and, while acting as if they believe in the purity of the young man, they actually do not believe in it.

"They know what must be held out to people for themselves and their daughters. We men sin through not knowing, and are determined not to learn. As for the women, they know very well that the noblest and most beautiful love depends, not on moral qualities, but on physical closeness, and also on the manner of doing the hair, and the color and shape.

"Ask an experienced woman practiced in leading men to sin which she would prefer, to be accused in the presence of the man whom she is engaged in trying to win over of being false, stubborn, or cruel, or to appear before him in an ill-fitting dress, or a dress of an ugly color?

"She will prefer the first. She knows very well that we simply lie when we talk of our high moral feelings, that we seek only the possession of her body. And that because of that we will forgive her every sort of bad behavior, but will not forgive her a dress of an ugly shade that is without taste or fit.

"And these things she knows by reason, where-as the young woman knows them only by feeling, like the animal. Thus these awful, tight-fitting clothes, these false shapes, these bare shoulders, arms, and throats.

"Women, especially those who have passed through the school of being married, know very well that conversations upon high subjects are only conversations, and that man seeks and desires the body, and all that makes the body pleasing. Thus, they act according to that belief.

"If we reject the usual reasons they give for their actions, and view the life of our upper and lower classes as it is, with all its hidden shame, it is only a vast lie.

"You do not share this opinion? Permit me, I am going to prove it to you (said he, interrupting me).

"You say that the women of our society have a different interest from that which moves fallen women to do what they do. And I say no, and I am going to prove it to you.

"If beings differ from one another according to the purpose of their life, according to their INNER LIFE, this will necessarily show also in their OUTER LIFE, and their outer life will be very different.

"Well, then, compare the unhappy woman, the looked-down-upon woman, with the women of the highest society: the same dresses, the same fashions, the same passion for jewelry, for bright and very expensive articles, the same dances, music, and songs.

"The former attract by all possible means; so do the latter. No difference, none whatever!

"Yes, and I, too, was caught by clothes, and curled hair."

Chapter VII

"And it was very easy to catch me, since I was brought up under false conditions, like vegetables in a hot-house.

"Too much food, together with our complete lack of exercise, does nothing but excite our desire. The men of our society are fed and kept like animals to make love.

"It is sufficient to close the out-let – that is, for a young man to live a quiet life for some time – to produce as an immediate result an uneasiness which, blown up by thought through our idle life, creates the false idea of love.

"All our ideas about being married are the result for the most part of our eating. Does that surprise you? For my part, I am surprised we do not see it.

"Not far from my home this spring, some laborers were working on a railway. You know what a worker's food is – bread, kvass***, onions. With this little food he lives, he is strong, he makes light work in the fields.

"On the railway this becomes a pound of meat. But the laborer uses this meat for sixteen hours of labor, pushing loads weighing twelve hundred pounds. And we, who eat two pounds of meat and game, who take in all sorts of heated drinks and food, how do we use it up? In sin.

"If the door to sin is open, all goes well. But close it, as I had closed it for a time before I got married, and immediately we become excited.

*** *kvass is a kind of cider*

And this, lied about by novels, poetry, and music, by our way of life, makes us imagine a love of the finest kind.

"I, too, fell in love, as everybody does, and there were flights of fancy, emotions, poetry, but really all this passion was prepared by mother and the dress makers.

"If there had been no trips in boats, no well-fitted clothes, and so on, if my wife had worn some ill-made clothes, and I had seen her thus at home, I should not have been taken in by her."

Chapter VIII

"Note, also, this falsity of which all are guilty; the way in which it is arranged for people to marry. What could be more natural? The young girl is of an age to be married; she should marry. What could be simpler, provided the young person is not too ugly, and men can be found with a desire to marry? Well, no, here begins a new lie.

"Formerly, when the young woman arrived at the right age, her becoming married was arranged by her parents. That was done, that is done still, through all humanity, among the Chinese, the Hindoos, the Mussulmans, and among our common people also.

"Things are so managed in at least ninety-nine per cent of the families of the entire human race. Only we who live in sin have imagined that this way was bad, and have invented another. And this other, what is it? It is this.

"The young girls are seated, and the gentlemen walk up and down before them as at a sale, and make their choice. The young women wait and think, but do not dare to say: 'Take me, young man, me and not her. Look at these shoulders and the rest.'

"We males walk up and down, and make a guess as to the worth of the women, and then we talk about the rights of woman, upon the liberty she has gained, I know not how, in the halls of the theaters."

"But what is to be done?" said I to him. "Shall the woman make the advances?"

"I do not know. But, if it is a question of equality, let the equality be complete. Though it has been found that to contract to marry through match-makers is shaming, it is nevertheless a thousand times preferable to our system.

"There, the rights and the chances are equal; here, the woman is a slave, displayed in the market. But as she cannot accept her condition, or take steps herself, there begins that other and worse lie, which is sometimes called GOING INTO SOCIETY, sometimes AMUSING ONE'S SELF, but which is really nothing but the hunt for a husband.

"Say to a mother or to her daughter that what they are doing is only hunting for a husband. God! What a hurt! Yet they can do nothing else, and have nothing else to do. The worst feature of it all is to see sometimes very young women with nothing but such ideas on their minds.

"If only, I repeat, it was done openly and honestly; but it is always accompanied with lies and talk of this sort:

"'The handing down of names! How interesting!'

"'Oh, Lily is much interested in painting.'

"'Shall you go to the Exposition? How charming!'

"'And the troika****, and the plays, and the music. Ah, how wonderful!'

"'My Lise has a passion for music.'

"And through all this talk, all have but one single idea: 'Take me, take my Lise. No, me! Only try!'"

**** *carriage drawn by three horses*

CHAPTER IX

"Do you know," Posdnicheff suddenly continued, "that this power of women from which the world suffers rises only from what I have just spoken of?"

"What do you mean by the power of women?" I said. "It's just the opposite. Everybody complains that women have not sufficient rights, that they are subjects."

"That's it; that's it exactly," said he, getting excited. "That is just what I mean, and that explains this odd state of affairs, that on the one hand woman is reduced to the lowest degree of shame, and on the other hand she rules over everything.

"See the Jews: with their power of money, they make up for their being subjected, just as the women do. 'You wish us to be only merchants? All right; staying only merchants, we will get possession of you,' say the Jews.

"'Ah! You wish us to be only objects of desire? All right; by the aid of desire we will force you to do our will,' say the women.

"The lack of the rights of woman does not consist in the fact that she has not the right to vote, or the right to decide the laws, but in the fact that in her love relations she is not the equal of man; she has not the right to choose instead of being chosen.

"You say that that would not be normal. Very well! But then do not let man enjoy these rights while his companion is without them and finds herself obliged to make use of her femaleness to govern, so that the result is that man chooses 'formally,' whereas really it is woman who chooses. As soon as she is in possession of her means, she abuses them, and gains a terrible upper hand."

"But where do you see this great power?"

"Where? Why, everywhere, in everything. Go see the stores in the large cities. There are millions there, millions. It is impossible to even guess the quantity of labor that is used there. In nine-tenths of these stores is there anything whatever for the use of men?

"All the rich things of life are demanded by woman. Count the factories; most of them are busy making things for women. Millions of men die working like slaves simply to satisfy the desires of our companions. Women, like queens, keep nine-tenths of the human race as prisoners of war, or as prisoners at hard labor. And all this because they have been shamed, because their rights, which should be equal to those men enjoy, are denied them. They take advantage of our desire for them; they catch us in their nets.

"Yes, the whole thing is there. Women have so armed themselves that a young man, and even an old man, cannot remain at ease in their presence. Watch a popular festival, or our parties or ball-rooms. Woman well knows her influence there. You will see it in her smiles of victory.

"As soon as a young man advances toward a woman, directly he falls under the influence of this desire and loses his head. Long ago I felt ill at ease when I saw a woman too well dressed, whether a woman of the people with her red cloth about her neck and her loose skirt, or a woman of our own society in her ball-room dress.

"Now it simply sends terror through me. I see in it a danger to men, something against the laws; and I feel a desire to call a policeman to defend me from this, to demand that this dangerous object be removed.

"And this is not a joke, by any means. I am sure the time will come – and perhaps it is not far distant – when the world will understand this, and will be surprised that a society could exist in which actions as harmful as those which appeal to desire by dressing the body, as our companions do, were allowed. Might as well put nets on our public streets to catch us, or worse than that."

CHAPTER X

"That, then, was the way in which I was caught. I was in love, as it is called. Not only did she appear to me a perfect being, but I considered myself a white black-bird.

"It is a well-known fact that there is no one so low in the world that he cannot find some one worse than himself, and thus blow himself up with pride and self-assurance. I was in that situation. I did not marry for money. Interest in money was foreign to the affair, unlike most of the men I knew, who married for money or for relations.

"First, I was rich, she was poor. Second, I was especially proud of the fact that, while others married with an intention of continuing their life as single men, it was my firm intention to be true to my wife before and after the wedding, and my pride swelled.

"Yes, I was a sinner, convinced that I was pure. The period of my being engaged did not last long. I cannot remember those days without shame. What a hated thing I was!

"It is generally agreed that love is moral, a community of thought rather than of sense. If that is the case, this community of thought ought to find expression in words and conversation.

"Nothing of the sort. It was very difficult for us to talk with each other. What a labor of Sisyphus was our conversation! Scarcely had we thought of something to say, and said it, when we had to fall silent again and try to discover new subjects. Literally, we did not know what to say to each other. All that we could think of concerning the life that was before us and our home was said.

"What then? If we had been animals, we should have known that we had not to talk. But, not being animals, it was necessary to talk, and there was nothing to talk about! For what occupied our minds was not a thing to be expressed in words.

"And then the custom of eating sweets, those terrible things we prepare for the wedding, those discussions with the mother upon the apartments, the sleeping-rooms, the bedding, upon the morning clothes, upon the wraps, the sheets, the dresses!

"Understand, if people married according to the old fashion, as this old man said just now, then these soft covers and this bedding would all be important details. But with us, out of ten married people there is scarcely to be found one who, I do not say believes in all these things (whether he believes or not does not matter to us), but believes in what he promises.

"Out of a hundred men, there is scarcely one who has not been married before, and out of fifty scarcely one who has made up his mind to be true to his wife. Most look upon this journey to the church as a condition necessary to the possession of a certain woman.

"Think then of the great meaning which material details must take on. Is it not a sort of sale, in which a young woman is given over to a sinner, the sale being surrounded with the most pleasant details?"

CHAPTER XI

"All marry in this way. And I did like the rest. If the young people who dream of the honey-moon only knew what a come-down it is, and always will be! I really do not know why all think it necessary to hide it.

"One day I was walking among the shows in Paris, when I saw a sign and entered a building to see a woman with hair on her face who claimed to be a man, and a dog said to live in the water. The woman was really a man, and the dog was an ordinary dog covered with a fish skin, swimming in a bath.

"It was not in the least interesting, but the Barnum accompanied me to the door very pleasantly, and, in addressing the people who were coming in, pointed to me and said: 'Ask the gentleman if it is not worth seeing! Come in, come in! It only costs a quarter!'

"Taken by surprise, I did not dare answer that there was nothing curious to be seen, and it was upon my false shame that the Barnum must have counted.

"It must be the same with the persons who have passed through the falsity of the honey-moon. They do not dare to tell their neighbor how false it all is. And I did the same.

"The happiness of the honey-moon does not exist. It is just the opposite; it is a period of being ill at ease, of shame, of pity, and, above all, of being terribly bored.

"It is something like the feeling of a youth when he first takes up cigarettes. He wants to throw up, but he draws in the smoke as if he enjoys this little 'pleasure'. The sin of marriage . . ."

"What! Sin?" I asked. "You are talking of one of the most natural things."

"Natural!" said he. "Natural! No, I consider it to be against nature, and it is I, a man who has sinned who has come to believe this. What would it be, then, if I had not known sin? To a young girl, to every pure young girl, it is an act that is quite not natural, just as it is to children.

"My sister married, when very young, a man twice her own age, who was utterly without morals. I remember how surprised we were the night of her wedding when, pale and covered with tears, she fled from her husband, her whole body trembling, saying that for nothing in the world would she tell what he wanted of her.

"You say natural? It is natural to eat; that is a pleasant act, which no one is shamed to perform from the time of his birth. No, it is not natural. A pure young girl wants one thing – children. Children, yes, not a lover." . . .

"But," said I, greatly surprised, "how would the human race continue?"

"What is the use of its continuing?" he answered.

"What! What is the use? But then we should not exist."

"And why is it necessary that we should exist?"

"Why, to live, to be sure."

"And why live? The Schopenhauers, the Hartmanns, and all the Buddhists, say that the greatest happiness is Nirvana, Non-Life; and they are right in this sense – that human happiness comes when we destroy our 'Self.' Only they do not express themselves well.

"They say that Humanity should destroy itself to avoid its sufferings, that its object should be to destroy itself. Now the object of Humanity cannot be to avoid sufferings by destroying ourselves, since suffering is the result of activity.

"The object of activity cannot consist in doing away with what it results in. The object of Man, as of Humanity, is happiness, and, to obtain it, Humanity has a law which it must carry out. This law consists in the uniting of human beings. This uniting is blocked by the passions. And that is why, if the passions disappear, the uniting will be accomplished. Humanity then will have carried out the law, and will have no further reason to exist."

"And before Humanity carries out the law?"

"In the meantime it will have the signs of the law not being fulfilled, and the existence of physical love. As long as this love exists, and because of it, many children will be born, until finally they fulfill the law.

"When at last the law shall be fulfilled, the Human Race will be done away with. At least it is impossible for us to imagine Life in the perfect uniting of people."

Chapter XII

"Strange theory!" cried I.

"Strange in what way? According to the teachings of the Church, the world will have an end. Science teaches the same. Why, then, is it strange that the same thing should result from moral Doctrine?

"'Let those who can, keep themselves pure, said Christ. And I take this sentence to mean exactly what it says. That morality may exist between people in this world, they must make complete purity their object. Toward this end, man must humble himself.

"When he shall reach the last degree of being humble, we shall be married in a way that is moral. But if man, as in our society, tends only toward physical love, though he may cover it with the false forms of being married, he will have only sin that is permitted. He will know only the same life without morals in which I fell, and caused my wife to fall, a life we call the honest life of the family.

"Think what odd ideas must rise when the happiest situation of man – liberty, purity – is looked upon as something terrible and strange. The highest ideal, the best situation of woman, to be pure, excites fear and laughter in our society.

"How many young girls give up their purity to this Moloch of opinion by being married to evil men that they may not remain pure – that is, superior! Through fear of finding themselves in that ideal state, they ruin themselves.

"But I did not understand this formerly. I did not understand that the words of the Gospel, that 'he who looks upon a woman to desire her has already sinned,' do not apply just to the wives of others, but especially to our own wives. I did not understand this.

"I thought that the honey-moon and all my acts during that period were virtues, and that to satisfy one's desires with his wife is a very pure thing to do.

"Know, then, that I consider these acts, which young married couples arrange with the permission of their parents, as nothing else than freedom to sin.

"I saw in this at the time nothing bad or shameful, and, hoping for great joys, I began to live the honey-moon. And though none of these joys followed, I had faith, and was determined to have them, cost what they might.

"But the more I tried to secure them, the less I succeeded. All this time I felt anxious, full of shame, and very tired.

"Soon I began to suffer. I believe that on the third or fourth day I found my wife sad and asked her the reason. I began to kiss her, which in my opinion was all that she could desire. But she pushed me away with her hand, and began to weep.

"At what? She could not tell me. She was filled with sorrow, with pain. Probably her nerves had suggested to her the truth about how base our relations were, but she found no words with which to say it.

"I began to question her; she answered that she missed her mother. It seemed to me that she was not telling the truth. I tried to make her feel better by keeping silent in regard to her parents. I did not imagine that she felt herself simply over-come with feelings, and that her parents had nothing to do with her sorrow.

"She did not listen to me, and I accused her of fancy. I began to laugh at her gently. She dried her tears, and began to blame me, in hard and wounding terms, for thinking only of myself, and for being cruel. I looked at her. Her whole face expressed hate, hate for me. I can't describe to you the fear this sight gave me.

" 'How? What?' thought I. 'Love is the unity of souls, and here she hates me? Me? Why? But it is impossible! It is no longer she!'

"I tried to calm her. I met with nothing but cold hate. Having no time to reflect, I was seized with anger. We exchanged hurting remarks.

"The impression of this first quarrel was terrible. I say quarrel, but the term is not exact. It was the sudden discovery of the huge wedge that had risen between us. Love was spent with the satisfaction of our physical needs. We stood face to face in our true light, like two people trying to get the greatest possible enjoyment by using each other.

"So what I called our quarrel was our actual situation as it appeared after the satisfaction of physical desire. I did not realize that this cold hate was our normal state, and that this first quarrel would soon be drowned under a new flood of desire.

"I thought that we had quarreled with each other, had made up, and that it would not happen again. But in this same honey-moon there came a period of having had enough of physical desire, in which we ceased to be necessary to each other, and a new quarrel broke out.

"It became plain that the first quarrel was not a matter of chance. 'It could not be avoided,' I thought. This second quarrel shocked me because it was based on a cause that was not just. It was something like a question of money, and never had I quarreled on that score; it was even impossible that I should do so in relation to her.

"I only remember that, in answer to some remark I made, she said I was trying to rule her by means of money, and that it was on money that I based my right over her. In short, something base, which was neither in my character nor in hers.

"I was beside myself. I accused her of being cruel. She accused me of being the same, and the quarrel broke out. In her words, in the look on her face, in her eyes, I noticed again the hate that had so shocked me before. With a brother, friends, my father, I had quarreled on occasion, but never had there been between us this fierce anger.

"Some time passed. Our hate for each other was again hidden by physical desire, and I made myself believe that these scenes were faults that could be repaired over time. But when they were repeated a third and a fourth time, I understood that they were not simply faults, but something that must happen again.

"I no longer felt fear. I was simply shocked that I should be the one to live in such an uncomfortable manner with my wife, and I was sure the same thing did not happen in other households. I did not know that in all households the same sudden changes take place; but that all, like myself, imagine it is something that they alone experience, which they carefully hide, not only to others, but to themselves, like a bad disease.

"That was what happened to me. Begun in the early days, it continued, and increased with a fury that also increased. From the first weeks, I felt that I was in a trap, that I had what I did not expect, and that being married is not a joy, but a painful trial.

"Like everybody else, I refused to speak about it (I should not have spoken about it even now but for what happened). Now I am shocked to think that I did not see my real situation. It was so simple that I should have seen it, in view of those quarrels, begun for reasons so common that afterwards one could not remember them.

"Just as it often happens among young people that, in the absence of jokes, they laugh at their own laughter, so we found no reasons for our hating. We hated each other because hate was naturally boiling up in us.

"Stranger still was the lack of causes for forgiving. Sometimes words, reasons, or even tears, but sometimes, I remember, after angry words, there followed kisses and talk of love. How terrible! Why is it I did not then see how base it was?"

CHAPTER XIII

"All of us, men and women, are brought up with the wrong ideas about this feeling we call love. From childhood I had prepared myself for this thing, and I loved during all my youth. I was joyous in loving. It had been put into my head that it was the noblest and highest occupation in the world.

"But when this expected feeling came at last, and I, a man, gave myself to it, the lie was revealed. In theory, a pure love is possible; in practice, love is a base and shaming thing, which is terrible to talk about and terrible to remember. But people make believe it is beautiful and right.

"I will tell you honestly and briefly what were the first signs of my love. I gave myself to animal-like acts. Not only was I not shamed by them, but I was proud of them, giving no thought to the mind and feelings of my wife. And not only did I not think of her mind or feelings, I did not even consider her physical life.

"I was shocked at the origin of our hate, and yet how clear it was! This hate is nothing but a protest of human nature against the animal in us that makes us slaves. It could not be otherwise. This hate was the hate of companions in a crime. Was it not a crime that, this poor woman having become with child the first month, our animal-like acts should have continued just the same?

"You imagine that I am wandering from my story. Not at all. I am giving you an account of the events that led to the murder of my wife. The fools! They think I killed my wife on the 5th of October. It was long before that that I destroyed her, just as husbands all kill their wives now.

"Understand well that in our society there is an idea shared by all, that woman gives man pleasure (and the other way round, probably, though I know nothing of that; I only know my own case).

"Wine, women, and song! So say the poets.

"If it were only that! Take all the poetry, the paintings, and the other arts, beginning with Pouschkine's 'Little Feet,' with 'Venus and Phryne,' and you will see that woman is only a means of pleasure.

"That is what she is at Trouba,***** at Gratchevka, and in a court ball-room. And think of this devil-like trick: if she were a thing without moral value, it might be said that woman is a fine piece. But men like this assure us that they look up to women (they look up to her, but also look upon her, however, as a means of pleasure).

"All assure us they respect women. Some give up their seats to her, pick up her handkerchief; others recognize her right to fill offices, take part in government, and so on, but the main point remains the same: She is, and remains, an object of physical desire, and she knows it.

"She is a slave, for a slave is nothing else than one who labors for the enjoyment of others, though they may not be called a slave. Actually, this is what happens.

"They do away with the external form, the formal sales of slaves, and then they imagine and assure others that slaves no longer exist. They are not willing to see that it still exists, since people, as before, like to profit by the labor of others, and think it good and just. This being given, there will always be found beings stronger or more clever than others to profit by it.

"The same thing happens in the freeing of woman. At bottom female servitude consists entirely in her association with a means of pleasure. Men excite woman, they give her all sorts of rights equal to those of men, but they continue to look upon her as an object of physical desire, and they bring her up in this manner from childhood, and in public opinion.

"She is always the base and ruined slave, and man remains always the terrible Master. Yes, to abolish slaves, public opinion must admit that to use one's neighbor for one's own gain is wrong, and, to make

***** *A suburb of Moscow*

woman free, public opinion must admit that it is a shame to consider her as a means of pleasure.

"The freedom of woman is not to be made in the public courts or in the political halls, but in the bedroom. Love for hire is to be fought, not in the houses of ill-fame, but in the family.

"They free woman in the public courts and in the halls of politics, but she remains an instrument of pleasure. Teach her, as she is taught among us, to look upon herself as such, and she will always remain a lesser being.

"Either, with the aid of doctors, she will try to prevent being with child, and go down, not to the level of an animal, but to the level of a thing; or she will be what she is in most cases – sick, mentally and physically, and without hope of getting better."

"But why that?" I asked.

"Oh! the most shocking thing is that no one is willing to see this, plain as it is. The doctors must understand this, but they take good care not to. Man does not wish to know the law of nature – to produce children. But children are born and become something that shames us.

"Man finds a means of avoiding this. We have not yet reached the low level of Europe, nor Paris, nor the 'system of two children,' nor Mahomet. We have discovered nothing, because we have given it no thought. We feel that there is something bad in the means we use; but we wish to preserve the family, and our view of woman is still worse.

"With us woman must be at the same time lover and nurse, and her strength is not sufficient. That is why we have attacks of nerves, and, among the lower classes, that which is not understood. Note that among the young girls of the lower classes this state of things does not exist, but only among the wives, and the wives who live with their husbands. The reason is clear, and this is the cause of the mental and moral decline of woman, and of her shame.

"If they would only realize what a grand work for the wife is the period of being with child! In her is forming the being who continues us, and this holy end is blocked and made painful . . . by what? It is terrible to think of it!

"And after that they talk of the liberties and the rights of woman! It is like making prisoners fat in order to eat them, and assuring them at the same time that their rights and their liberties are guarded!"

All this was new to me, and shocked me very much.

"But if this is so," said I, "it follows that one may love his wife only once every two years; and as man…"

"And as man has need of her, you are going to say. At least, so the scientists assure us. I would force them to fulfill the purpose of these women who, in their opinion, are necessary to man.

"I wonder what song they would sing then. Assure man that he needs wine and pain-killers, and he will believe those poisons necessary.

"It follows that God did not know how to arrange matters properly, since, without asking the opinions of the scientists, he has made things as they are. Man needs, so they have decided, to satisfy his physical desire, and the birth and the nursing of children gets in the way of this.

"What, then, is to be done? Why, apply to the scientists; they will arrange everything, and they have really discovered a way.

"When will these men with their lies have their crowns removed! It is high time. We have had enough of them. People go mad, and shoot each other, and always because of that! How could it be otherwise?

"One would say that the animals know that having off-spring continues their race, and that they follow a certain law in that regard. Only man does not know this, and is not willing to know it. He cares only to have as much physical pleasure as possible. The king of nature – man!

"In the name of love he kills half the human race. Of woman, who ought to be his aid in the movement of humanity toward liberty, he makes, in the name of his pleasures, not an aid, but an enemy.

"Who is it that everywhere puts a check upon the forward movement of humanity? Woman. Why is it so? For the reason that I have given, and for that reason only."

CHAPTER XIV

"Yes, much worse than an animal is man when he does not live as a man. Thus was I. The terrible part is that I believed, since as I had nothing to do with other women, that I was leading an honest family life, that I was a very moral being, and that if we had quarrels, the fault was in my wife, and in her character.

"But it is plain that the fault was not in her. She was like most everybody else. She was brought up according to the principles of our society—that is, as all the young girls of our wealthy classes, without exception, are brought up, and as they cannot fail to be brought up.

"How many times we hear or read of thoughts upon the condition of women, and upon what they ought to be. But these are only vain words. The education of women results from the real and not imagined view which the world holds of women's place in life.

"According to this view, the condition of women consists in giving pleasure, and it is to that end that her education is directed. From her birth she is taught only those things that are meant to increase her charm. Every young girl is used to thinking only of that.

"As slaves were brought up only to please their masters, so woman is brought up to please men. It cannot be otherwise.

"But you will say, perhaps, that that applies only to young girls who are badly brought up, that there is another education, an education that is serious, in the schools, an education in the dead languages, an education in courses on medicine, and in other courses.

"It is false. Every sort of female education has for its object the pleasing of men. In some it is by music or curled hair, in others by science or social good. The object is the same, and cannot be otherwise (since no other object exists) – to win a man in order to possess him.

"Imagine courses of instruction for women and female science without men – that is, learned women, and men not KNOWING them as learned. Oh, no! It is not possible. No education, no instruction can change woman as long as her highest ideal is to be married, and not purity, freedom from physical desire.

"Until that time she will remain a slave. One need only imagine, forgetting how wide-spread the case is, the conditions in which our young girls are brought up, to avoid being shocked at the lack of morality of the women of our upper classes. It is the opposite, morality in upper class women: *that* would cause us to be shocked.

"Follow my reasoning. With their complete lack of exercise, too much care of the body, and a great eating of sweets, and God knows how the poor women suffer from the desires of their own bodies, excited by all these things.

"Nine out of ten are pained by desire during the first period of being adult, and afterward if they do not marry at the age of twenty. That is what we are not willing to see, though those with eyes to see, see it all the same.

"Most of these poor women are so excited by hidden desires (and it is lucky if it is hidden) that they are fit for nothing. They come to life only in the presence of men. Their whole life is spent in preparing themselves for men. In the company of men they become excited; they begin to live by energy of their desires. But the moment the man goes away, the life stops.

"And that is not when they are with a certain man, but when they are with any man, if he is not completely ugly. You will say that this is an exception. No, it is a rule. Only in some it is made very plain, in other less so. But no one lives by her own life; they all depend upon man.

"They cannot be otherwise, since to them being noticed by the greatest number of men is the ideal of life (both for young girls and married women). It is for this reason they have no feeling stronger than that of the animal need of every female who tries to attract the largest number of males in order to increase the opportunities for choice.

"So it is in the life of young girls, and so it continues after being married. In the life of young girls it is necessary in order to select, and when married it is necessary in order to rule the husband.

"Only one thing stops or slows this for a time – namely, children – and then only when the woman is not completely evil – that is, when she nurses her own children. But here again the doctor gets into the act.

"With my wife, who desired to nurse her own children, and who did nurse six of them, it happened that the first child was sickly. The doctors, who took off her clothes and felt of her everywhere, and whom I had to thank and pay for these acts, these dear doctors decided that she ought not to nurse her child, and she, for a time, had the only remedy for her need for men taken away.

"A wet-nurse finished the nursing of this first-born – that is to say, we profited by the need for money of a poor woman to steal her from her own little one in favor of ours.

"Nevertheless, that is not the question. There was again stirred up in my wife that need for men which had been sleeping during the nursing period. Thanks to that, she woke in me once again the pain of not trusting her that I had formerly known, though in a much slighter degree."

CHAPTER XV

"Yes, not trusting your partner is another of the secrets of being married that is known to all and concealed by all. Besides the general cause of the hate of husbands and wives resulting from joining in spoiling what it means to be a human being, and also from other causes, the never-ending source of wounds lies in the lack of trust.

"But it is determined to hide them from all, and we hide them. Knowing them, each one supposes in himself that it is his fault, and not a common fault. So it was with me, and it had to be so.

"There cannot fail to be lack of trust between husbands and wives who live lives that are not moral. If they cannot give up their pleasures for the sake of their child, they conclude from that, and truly, that they will not give up their pleasures for, I will not say happiness and peace (since one may sin in secret), but even for the sake of their peace of mind.

"Each one knows very well that neither admits any high moral reasons for not calling the other to task, since in their personal relations they fail in the morality required, and from that time they lack trust and keep a close watch each on the other.

"Oh, what a terrible feeling is lack of trust! I do not speak of that real lack of trust which has foundations (it is painful, but it promises an issue), but of that lack of trust which always accompanies being married when it is not moral, and which, having no cause, has no end.

"This lack of trust is fearful. Fearful, that is the word. Here's an example: A young man speaks to my wife. He looks at her with a smile and, as it seems to me, he looks at her body. How does he dare to think

46

of her, to think of the possibility of making love to her? And how can she, seeing this, put up with him?

"Not only does she put up with him, but she seems pleased. I even see that she puts herself to trouble on his account. And in me there rises such a hate for her that each of her words, each gesture, turns my stomach. She notices it, she knows not what to do, and assumes an air of not being aware of it.

"Ah! I suffer! That makes her gay, she is content. And my hate increases ten-fold, but I do not dare to show it, because at bottom I know that there are no real reasons for it, and I remain in my seat, pretending not to care and increasing my attention and being more pleasant to HIM.

"Then I get angry with myself. I desire to leave the room, to leave them alone, and I do, in fact, go out; but scarcely am I out when I have a fear of what is taking place in my absence. I go in again, making up some excuse. Or sometimes I do not go in; I remain near the door, and listen.

"How can she shame herself and shame me by placing me in this terrible situation of suspecting and looking on without being noticed? Oh, hated act! Oh, the evil animal! And he, too, what does he think of you?

"But he is like all men. He is what I was before I married. It gives him pleasure. He even smiles when he looks at me, as much as to say: 'What have you to do with this? It is my turn now.'

"This feeling is terrible. It cannot be endured. To have this feeling toward anyone, to once suspect a man of wanting to sleep with my wife, was enough to spoil this man forever in my eyes. Let me once suspect another man, and never more could I keep up simple human relations with him, and my eyes flashed when I looked at him.

"As for my wife, so many times had I looked at her with this moral poison, with this hate, that she was lowered in my eyes. In the periods of this hate without cause I gradually removed her crown.

"I covered her with shame in my mind. I invented impossible evils. I suspected, I feel shame to say, that she, this queen of 'The Thousand and One Nights,' cheated on me under my very eyes, and laughed at me.

"Thus, each new time I suspected her (I speak always of suspecting her without cause), I entered into the hole dug formerly when I suspected her, and I continued to deepen it. She did the same thing.

"If I had reasons to suspect her, she who knew my past had a thousand times more reasons. And she was more ill-natured about it than I. And the sufferings that I felt from her suspecting me were different, and very painful.

"The situation may be described thus: We are living more or less at peace. I am even gay and contented. Suddenly we start a conversation on some most common-place subject, and right away she finds herself not agreeing with me upon matters about which we have been generally in agreement. And also I see that, without any reason for it, she is becoming angry.

"I think that she is having an attack of nerves, or else that the subject of conversation is really not agreeable to her. We talk of something else, but it begins again.

"Again she flies at me, and becomes angry. I am shocked and look for a reason. Why? For what? She keeps silent, or gives me short answers, mentioning other things.

"I begin to guess that the reason of all this is that I have taken a few walks in the garden with her cousin, to whom I did not give even a thought. I begin to guess, but I cannot say so. If I say so, I make it certain that what she suspects is true.

"I question her. She does not answer, but she sees that I understand, and that makes what she suspects true.

"'What is the matter with you?' I ask.

"'Nothing, I am as well as usual,' she answers.

"At the same time, like a crazy woman, she makes remarks that don't make sense, exploding with anger.

"Sometimes I am patient, but at other times I get angry. Then she explodes in a flood of hurts, in charges of crimes she has imagined, all carried to the highest degree by weeping, tears, and running through the house to the most unlikely spots.

"I go to look for her. I feel shame before people, before the children, but there is nothing to be done. She is in a condition where I feel that she is ready for anything, and I am afraid of what she might do.

"I run, and finally find her hiding in her room.

"Nights of argument follow, in which both of us, nerves spent, finally calm each other after exchanging the most cruel and accusing words.

"Yes, lack of trust, without cause, is the condition of our morally wrong married life. And throughout my married life never did I cease to feel it and to suffer from it.

"There were two periods in which I suffered the most. The first time was after the birth of our first child, when the doctors would not let my wife nurse it.

"I was without trust, in the first place, because my wife felt that restlessness that animals feel when the regular course of life is interrupted without cause.

"But especially was I without trust because, having seen with what ease she had thrown off her moral duties as a mother, I concluded rightly that she would throw off as easily her duties as a wife, feeling all the surer of this because she was in perfect health, as was shown by the fact that she nursed her following children, and did it very well."

"I see that you have no love for the doctors," said I, having noticed Posdnicheff's sour expression and tone of voice whenever he spoke of them.

"It is not a question of loving them or of not loving them. They have ruined my life, as they have ruined the lives of thousands of beings before me, and I cannot help connecting the results with the cause. I believe that they desire, like the lawyers and the rest, to make money.

"I would willingly have given them half of my income – and any one would have done it in my place, understanding what they do – if they had consented to leave my married life alone, and to keep themselves at a distance.

"I have no facts, but I know scores of cases – in reality, they are without end – where they have killed, now a child in its mother's womb, saying without doubt that the mother could not give birth to it (when the mother could have given birth to it very well), now mothers through a so-called operation. No one has counted these murders, just as no one counted the murders of the Inquisition, because it was supposed that they were done for the benefit of humanity.

"Many are the crimes of the doctors! But all these crimes are nothing compared with the lack of morals they introduce into the world through women. I say nothing of the fact that, if it were to follow their advice – thanks to the sicknesses they see everywhere – humanity, instead of tending to unity, would proceed straight to complete lack of unity. Everybody, according to their belief, should separate himself.

"But I would pass over all these things. The most important poison is the false thinking of people, especially of women. One can no longer say now: 'You live badly, live better.' One can no longer say it either to himself or to others, for if you live badly (say the doctors), the cause is in the nerves, or in something similar, and it is necessary to go to see them, and they will give you a slip for thirty-five dollars' worth of cures to be bought at the drug-store, and you must take them. Your condition grows worse? Again to the doctors, and more cures! An excellent business!

"But to return to our subject. I was saying that my wife nursed her children well, that the nursing and the growth of the children, and the children in general, quieted my lack of trust, but that, on the other hand, they created pain of a different sort."

Chapter XVI

"The children came rapidly, one after another, and there happened what happens in our society with children and doctors. Yes, children, a mother's love, it is a painful thing.

"Children, to a woman of our society, are not a joy, a pride, nor a fulfilling of herself as a woman, but a cause of fear, anxiety, and suffering. Women say it, they think it, and they feel it too.

"Children to them are really a suffering, not because they do not wish to give birth to them, nurse them, and care for them (women with a strong need to mother – and such was my wife – are ready to do that), but because the children may fall sick and die.

"They do not wish to give birth to them, and then not love them; and when they love, they do not wish to feel fear for the child's health and life. That is why they do not wish to nurse them.

"'If I nurse it,' they say, 'I shall become too fond of it.' One would think that they preferred dolls as children, which could neither be sick nor die, and could always be repaired. How mixed up are the brains of these poor women! Why such awful acts to avoid being with child, and to avoid the love of the little ones?

"Love, the condition of most joy for a woman, appears as a danger. And why? Because, when a man does not live as a man, he is worse than a beast.

"A woman cannot look upon a child otherwise than as a pleasure. It is true that it is painful to give birth to it, but what little hands! . . . Oh, the little hands! Oh, the little feet! Oh, its smile! Oh, its little body! Oh, its baby talk! In a word, it is the feeling of mothering an animal has.

51

"But as for any idea as to the meaning of the appearance of a new human being to take our place, there is scarcely a sign of it. Nothing of it appears in all that is said and done. No one has any faith now in raising a child in the church, and yet that was but a reminder of the human importance of the new-born baby.

"They have thrown all that aside, but they have not found anything to take its place, and there remain only the dresses, the little hands, the little feet, and whatever exists in the animal. But the animal has neither the ability to imagine, nor the ability to look ahead, nor reason, nor a doctor. No! Not even a doctor!

"The chicken drops its head, over-come, when its baby dies; or the baby cow dies and the cow drops its head; the hen and the cow sorrow for a time, and then these beasts continue to live, forgetting what has happened.

"With us, if the child falls sick, what is to be done, how to care for it, what doctor to call, where to go? If it dies, there will be no more little hands or little feet, and then what is the use of the sufferings endured?

"The cow does not ask all that, and this is why children are a source of suffering. The cow cannot imagine, and for that reason cannot think how it might have saved the child if it had done this or that, and its grief, founded in its physical being, lasts but a very short time.

"It is only a condition, and not that sorrow which becomes blown up to the point of despair, thanks to a shallow life. The cow has not that power to reason, which would make it possible to ask why. Why endure all these sufferings? What was the use of so much love, if the little ones were to die?

"The cow has no ability to reason which tells it to have no more children, and, if any come, to neither love nor nurse them, that it may not suffer. But our wives reason, and reason in this way, and that is why I said that, when a man does not live as a man, he is beneath the animal."

"But then, how is it necessary to act, in your opinion, in order to treat children in a human way?" I asked.

"How? Why, love them as a human."

"Well, do not mothers love their children?"

"They do not love them as a human, or very seldom do, and that is why they do not love them, even as dogs. Mark this, a chicken, a goose, a wild animal, will always remain true to ideals of animal love they cannot reach.

"It is a rare thing for a woman to throw herself, at the peril of her life, upon an elephant to save her child, whereas a chicken or a bird will not fail to fly at a dog and give its own life for its children.

"Observe this, also.

"Woman has the power to limit her physical love for her children, which an animal cannot do. Does that mean that, because of this, woman is less than the animal? No. She is superior (and even to say superior is not just, she is not superior, she is different), but she has other duties, human duties.

"She can control herself in the matter of animal love, and give her love instead to bettering the child. That is what woman's role should be, and that is just what we do not see in our society. We read of the heroic acts of mothers who give up their children in the name of a superior idea, and these things seem to us like tales of former times, which do not concern us.

"And yet I believe that, if the mother has not some ideal, in the name of which she can give up the animal feeling, and if this force finds no use, she will transfer it to vain attempts to physically preserve her child, helped in this task by the doctor, and she will suffer as she does suffer.

"So it was with my wife. Whether there was one child or five, the feeling remained the same. In fact, it was little better when there had been five. Life was always poisoned with fear for the children, not only from their real or imagined diseases, but even by their simple presence.

"For my part, at least through all of my married life, all my interests and all my happiness depended upon the health of my children, their condition, and their studies.

"Children, it is not necessary to say, should be taken seriously. But we all have a right to live, and in our days parents can no longer live. Regular life does not exist for them. The whole life of the family hangs by a hair.

"What a terrible thing it is to suddenly receive the news that little Basile is throwing up, or that Lise has a pain in the stomach! Right away you give up everything, you forget everything, everything becomes nothing. The important thing is the doctor, the cures, the temperature.

"You cannot begin a conversation but little Pierre comes running in with an anxious air to ask if he may eat an apple, or what jacket he shall put on, or else it is the nurse maid who enters with a screaming baby.

"Regular, steady family life does not exist. Where you live, and what you do, depends upon the health of the little ones, the health of the little ones depends upon nobody, and, thanks to the doctors, who pretend to aid health, your entire life is troubled.

"It is always a peril. Scarcely do we believe ourselves out of it when a new danger comes: more attempts to save. Always the situation of sailors on a sinking ship.

"Sometimes it seemed to me that this was done on purpose, that my wife made herself anxious in order to get the better of me, since that solved the question so simply for her benefit. It seemed to me that all she did at those times was done for its effect upon me.

"But now I see that she herself, my wife, suffered on account of the little ones, their health, and their diseases. It was painful to both of us, but to her the children were also a means of forgetting herself, like being drunk.

"I often noticed, when she was very sad, that she got relief when a child fell sick, at being able to find escape in this. It was a natural thing to do, because as yet there was nothing else.

"On every side we heard that Mrs. So-and-so had lost children, that Dr. So-and-so had saved the child of Mrs. So-and-so, and that in a certain family all had moved from the house in which they were living, and thus saved the little ones.

"And the doctors, with a serious air, said this was so, backing my wife in her opinions. She was not given to fear, but the doctor dropped some word that indicated a sickness, and off she went.

"It was impossible for it to be otherwise.

"Women in the old days had the belief that 'God has given, God has taken away,' that the little angel is going to heaven, and that it is better to die innocent than to die in sin.

"If the women of today had something like this faith, they could endure more peacefully the sickness of their children. But of all that there does not remain even a trace.

"And yet it is necessary to believe in something; so they believe in medicine, and not even in medicine, but in the doctor. One believes in X, another in Z, and, like all believers, they do not see how foolish their beliefs are.

"Their beliefs are foolish because, in reality, if they did not believe in a foolish way, they would see that what all these doctors recommend for them is in vain.

"When one lives in a large city, half the family has to move away from its home (we did it twice) when there is a disease around that one can catch, and yet every man in the city is a center through which pass all sorts of diseases. I would say that everyone who moves on account of disease will find in his new place another disease that is similar, if not the same.

"But that is not all. Every one knows rich people who, after a case of disease, destroy everything in their homes, and then fall sick in houses newly built and with new furniture. Every one knows, likewise, numbers of men who come in contact with sick people and do not get sick. Our anxieties are due to the people who pass on tall stories.

"One woman says that she has an excellent doctor. 'Pardon me,' answers the other, 'he killed such a one,' or such a one. Bring her another doctor, who knows no more, who learned from the same books, who treats illnesses the same way, but who goes about in a carriage, and asks a hundred rubles a visit, and she will have faith in him.

"It all lies in the fact that our women know nothing. They have no belief in God, but some of them believe in the evil eye, and the others in doctors who charge high fees. If they had faith they would know that even the worst diseases are not so terrible, since they cannot disturb that which man can and should love – the inner being.

"There can result from them only that which none of us can avoid – disease and death. Without faith in God, they love only physically, and all their energy is centered upon preserving life, which cannot be preserved, and which the doctors promise the fools of both sexes to save.

"And from that time there is nothing to be done; the doctors must be called. Thus the presence of the children not only did not improve our relations as husband and wife, but had the opposite effect.

The children became an added cause of quarrels, and the larger the children grew, the more they became an instrument of struggle.

"One would have said that we used them as weapons with which to fight each other. Each of us had his favorite. I made use of little Basile (the eldest), she of Lise. Further, when the children reached an age where their characters began to be set, they became our friends, whom we drew each in his or her own direction.

"They suffered terribly from this, the poor things, but we, always fighting, were not clear-headed enough to think of them. The little girl was devoted to me, but the eldest boy, who looked like my wife and was her favorite, often filled me with hate."

CHAPTER XVII

"We lived at first in the country, then in the city, and, if the final ill-fortune had not happened, I should have lived thus until my old age and should have believed that I had had a good life – not too good, but, on the other hand, not bad, an existence such as other people lead.

"I should not have understood the ill-fortune and base falsity in which I lived, feeling that something was not right. I felt, in the first place, that I, a man who, according to my ideas, ought to be the master, wore the dresses, and that I could not get rid of them.

"The principal cause of my being subjected was the children. I should have liked to free myself, but I could not. Bringing up the children, and resting upon them, my wife ruled. I did not then realize that she could not help ruling, especially because, in being married, she was morally superior to me, as every young girl is superior to the man, since she is so much purer.

"Strange thing! The ordinary wife in our society is a very common person or worse – self-centered, speaking badly of others, changing her mind without cause, where the ordinary young girl, until the age of twenty, is a charming being, ready for everything that is beautiful and high-minded. Why is this so? No doubt because husbands ruin them, and bring them down to their own level.

"In truth, if boys and girls are born equal, the little girls find themselves in a better situation. In the first place, the young girl is not subjected to the evil conditions to which we are subjected. She has neither cigarettes, nor wine, nor cards, nor companions, nor public houses, nor public affairs.

"But the chief thing is that she is physically pure, and that is why, in being married, she is superior to her husband. She is superior to man as a young girl, and when she becomes a wife in our society, where there is no need to work in order to live, she becomes superior, also, by the seriousness of the acts of giving birth, and nursing.

"Woman, in bringing a child into the world, and giving it her breast, sees clearly that her affair is more serious than the affair of man, who sits in the Zemstvo, in the court. She knows that in these affairs the main thing is money, and money can be made in different ways.

"For that reason money is not always necessary, like nursing a child. As a result, woman is superior to man, and must rule.

"But man, in our society, not only does not recognize this, but looks down upon her from the height of his position, and looks down on what she does.

"Thus my wife looked down on me for my work at the Zemstvo because she gave birth to children and nursed them. I, in turn, thought that woman's labor was the lowest, which one might and should laugh at. Apart from that and the other reasons, we were also separated by a hate for one another.

"It grew ever stronger, and we arrived at that period when, not only did lack of agreement increase the hate, but the hate caused the arguments. Whatever she might say, I was sure in advance to hold an opposite opinion; and she the same.

"Toward the fourth year of our being married it was quietly decided between us that no community of mind was possible, and we made no further attempts at it. As to the simplest objects, we each held strongly to our own opinions. With strangers we talked upon the most varied and most personal matters, but not with each other.

"Sometimes, in listening to my wife talk with others, I said to myself: 'What a woman! Everything that she says is a lie!' And I was shocked that the person with whom she was talking did not see that she was lying. When we were together, we kept silent, or to talk which, I am sure, might have been carried on by animals.

"'What time is it? It is bed-time. What is there for dinner to-day? Where shall we go? What is there in the newspaper? The doctor must be sent for, Lise has a sore throat.'

"Unless we kept within the extremely narrow limits of such conversation, arguments were sure to follow. The presence of a third person relieved us, for through such a person we could still talk to one another. She probably believed that she was always right. As for me, in my own eyes, I was perfect beside her.

"The periods of what we call love arrived as often as formerly. They were more animal-like, without being delicate or having any taste; but they were short, and were generally followed by periods of anger without cause, anger fed by the most slight of reasons.

"We had arguments about the coffee, the table-cloth, card games – the most minute things, in short, which could not be of the least importance to either of us.

"As for me, a terrible hate was always boiling up within me. I watched her pour the tea, swing her foot, lift her spoon to her mouth, and blow upon hot liquids or sip them, and I hated her as if these had been so many crimes.

"I did not notice that these periods of anger depended very regularly upon the periods of love. Each of the latter was followed by one of the former. A period of intense love was followed by a long period of anger; a period of mild love was cause for a mild anger.

"We did not understand that this love and this hate were two opposite faces of the same animal feeling. To live thus would be terrible, if one understood it. But we did not see this, we did not understand it.

"It is at once the pain and the relief of man that, when he lives in a way that is not normal, he can have ideas that are not true as to the pains of his situation. So did we.

"She tried to forget herself in occupations, in household duties, the care of the furniture, her dress and that of her children, in the education of the latter, and in looking after their health.

"These were occupations that did not rise from any immediate necessity, but she did them as if her life and that of her children depended on whether the cake was allowed to burn, whether a curtain was hanging properly, whether a dress was a success, whether a lesson was well learned, or whether a medicine was taken.

"I saw clearly that to her all this was, more than anything else, a means of forgetting, a drug, just as hunting, card-playing, and my duties at the Zemstvo served the same purpose for me. It is true that, in addition, I had an actual drug – cigarettes, which I smoked in large quantities, and wine, upon which I did not get drunk, but of which I took too much. I had drink before meals, and during meals two glasses of wine, so that the troubles of life were softened out of existence.

"These new theories of mental illness we hear about, that it's all in the mind, are not simply wrong, but dangerous or evil. Charcot, I am sure, would have said that my wife was out of her mind, and of me he would have said that I was not a normal being, and he would have wanted to treat me. But in us there was nothing requiring treatment.

"All this mental illness was the simple result of the fact that we were living a life without morals. Thanks to this kind of life, we suffered, and to cure our sufferings we tried means that were not normal, which the doctors call the 'indications' of a mental illness.

"There was no occasion in all this to apply for treatment to Charcot or to anybody else. No 'suggestion' would have been effective in working our cure. What was needed was someone to examine the origin of the evil.

"It is as when one is sitting on a nail; if you see the nail, you see that which is not regular in your life, and you avoid it. Then the pain stops, without any necessity of 'curing' it.

Our pain arose from the fact that we were not living a regular life. In my case it also rose from my lack of trust, my anger, and the need for keeping myself always in a state of being partially drugged by hunting, card-playing, and, above all, the use of wine and cigarettes.

"It was because our lives were not regular that my wife took up her occupations with such passion. Her sudden changes from extreme sadness to extreme gayness, her always talking, rose from the need to forget herself, and her life, through her many varied and brief occupations.

"Thus we lived lives in which we did not know our true condition. We were like two slaves fastened to the same oar in a boat, cursing each other, poisoning each other's existence, and trying to shake each other off.

"I was still not aware that ninety-nine families out of every hundred live in the same hell, and that it cannot be otherwise. I had not learned this fact from others or from myself. The strange things that are met in a regular life, and even in life that is not regular, are surprising.

"At the very time when the lives of the parents become impossible, it becomes necessary that they go to the city to live, in order to educate their children. That is what we did."

Posdnicheff became silent, and twice there escaped him, in the half-darkness, sounds which, at that moment, seemed to me like soft cries. Then he continued.

CHAPTER XVIII

"So we lived in the city. In the city those who are not happy feel less sad. One can live there a hundred years without being noticed, and be dead a long time before anybody will notice it.

"People have no time to ask you about your life. All are wrapped up in themselves. Their business, social relations, art, the health of children, their education. And there are visits that must be received and made; it is necessary to see this one, it is necessary to hear that one or the other one. In the city, also, there are always one, two, or three well-known people one must visit.

"Now one must care for himself, or care for such or such a little one, now it is the professor, the private teacher, those who look after the children . . . and our lives are absolutely empty. But in this activity we thought less of the sufferings of our living together.

"Moreover, in moving to the city we had a great occupation – the arranging of the new apartment, and then, too, the moving from the city to the country, and from the country to the city. Thus we spent a winter.

"The following winter something happened to us which passed without notice, but which was the basic cause of all that happened later. My wife was suffering, and the doctors would not permit her to have a child. They even taught her how to avoid it.

"I was very much against their thinking, and struggled vainly against their ideas, but she insisted, and I surrendered. Thus the last reason for living together as a married couple was taken from us, and life became baser than ever.

"The common working people need children, and thus there is a need for them to be married. But we, when we have a few children, have no need of any more. We do not see the need to explain away this lack of children. We have no sense of guilt left, except, so to speak, that occasioned by public opinion and the criminal code.

"But in this matter neither of these apply. There is no one in society who is shamed by it. Each one practices it. What's the use of having more children and taking from us the joys of social life?

"There is no reason to feel guilty, or fear the criminal code. Low girls, soldiers' wives who throw their children into ponds or wells, these certainly must be put in prison. But with us, the doing away with children is effected in a timely and proper manner.

"Thus we passed two years more. The method for not having children that was advised by the doctors had succeeded. My wife had put on weight and grown more handsome. It was the beauty of the end of summer.

"She felt it, and paid much attention to her person. She had become that beauty that stirs men. She had all the brightness of the wife of thirty years who has no children, eats heartily, and is excited. The very sight of her was enough to make one afraid. She was like a horse that has long been without a carriage to pull, and suddenly finds itself free of all controls.

"As for my wife, she had nothing to keep her in check; as for that matter, ninety-nine hundredths of our women have none."

CHAPTER XIX

Posdnicheff's face had changed; his eyes were something to pity; their expression seemed strange, like that of another being; his nose was smaller, his mouth larger, immense, fearful.

"Yes," he went on, "she had put on weight since she stopped having children, and her anxieties about her children began to disappear.

"One would have said she was waking from a long dream, that on coming to herself she saw the entire world with its joys, a whole world in which she had not learned to live, and which she did not understand.

"'If only this world shall not disappear! When time is past, when old age comes, one cannot recover it.'

"This I believe she thought, or rather felt. But how could she think or feel otherwise? She had been brought up with this idea that there is in the world but one thing worthy of attention – love.

"In getting married, she had known something of this love, but it was very far from everything that she had understood as promised her, everything that she expected. How much wrong thinking! How much suffering! And a suffering not expected – the children!

"This suffering had told upon her, and then, thanks to the obliging doctor, she had learned that it is possible to avoid having children. That had made her glad. She had tried, and she was now ready for the only thing that she knew – love.

"But love with a husband spoiled by lack of trust and ill-nature was no longer her ideal. She began to think of some other tenderness;

at least, that is what I thought. She looked about her as if expecting some event or some being. I noticed it, and I could not help being anxious.

"Always, now, it happened that, in talking with me through a third party (that is, in talking with others, but with the intention that I should hear), she boldly expressed – not thinking that an hour before she had said the opposite – half joking, half seriously, this idea that anxieties about mothering are a mistake; that it is not worth while to give up one's life to children.

"When one is young, it is necessary to enjoy life. So she occupied herself less with the children, not with the same seriousness as before, and paid more and more attention to herself, to her face – although she concealed it – to her pleasures, and even to her perfection from the worldly point of view.

"She began to devote herself with passion to the piano, which had formerly stood forgotten in the corner. There, at the piano, began the adventure.

"The MAN appeared."

Posdnicheff seemed shamed in speaking thus, and twice again there escaped him that strange sound of which I spoke above, as of a cry. I thought that it gave him pain to refer to the MAN, and to remember him. He made an effort, as if to break down whatever it was that shamed him, and continued with strength of will.

"He was a bad man in my eyes, not because he played such an important role in my life, but because he was really such. For the rest, from the fact that he was bad, we must conclude that he was not a responsible person.

"He was a musician, one who played the violin. Not one who earned his living that way, but half man of the world, half artist. His father, who had a place in the country, was a neighbor of my father's.

"The father had become ruined, and the children, three boys, were all sent away. Our man, the youngest, was sent to his god-mother at Paris. There they placed him in the Conservatory, for he showed a taste for music. He learned to play the violin, and played publicly."

On the point of speaking evil of the other, Posdnicheff checked himself, stopped, and said suddenly: "In truth, I know not how he lived. I only know that that year he came to Russia, and came to see me.

"He had eyes that always seemed to be wet with tears, smiling red lips, and a little hair on the upper lip. The hair on his head was brushed in the latest fashion.

"He had a pretty face – what the women call 'not bad', but was weakly built physically, with a body as broad as a woman's. He was correct in his manners, assuming a familiarity with people as far as possible, but had that sharp sense that quickly detects a false step and backs away.

"He was a man, in short, who observes the outer rules of dignity, with that special Parisianism that is revealed in buttoned shoes, a loud tie, and that something which foreigners pick up in Paris, and which, in its oddness and newness, always has an influence on our women.

"In his manners there was a false gayness, a way, you know, of saying everything by suggestion, not finishing what he begins, as if everything he says he thinks you know already, or would remember, and could supply what he fails to say.

"Well, he, with his music, was the cause of all.

"At the trial the affair was so represented that everything, it seemed, could be blamed on my jealousy.

"That is false – that is, not quite false, but there was something else. The decision of the trial was that I, a deceived husband, had killed in defense of my honor (that is the way they put it in their language), and thus I was declared not guilty.

"I tried to explain the affair from my own point of view, but they concluded that I simply wanted to protect the memory of my wife. Her relations with the musician, whatever they may have been, are now of no importance to me or to her. The important part is what I have told you.

"The whole tragedy was due to the fact that this man came into our house at a time when a huge divide already existed between my wife and myself, as well as that terrible tension of hate, in which the slightest excuse was enough to set off a crisis..

"Our quarrels in the last days were something terrible, and the more shocking because they were followed by an animal-like passion that was very strained.

"If it had not been he, some other would have come. If the excuse had not been lack of trust, I should have found another. I insist upon this point, that all husbands who live a married life like I lived, must either turn to outside sin, or separate from their wives, or kill themselves or their wives, as I did.

"If there is any man in my situation to whom this does not happen, he is a very rare exception. For, before ending the affair as I ended it, I was several times on the point of killing myself; and my wife made several attempts to poison herself."

CHAPTER XX

"So that you may understand me, I must tell you how this happened.

"We were living along in our fashion, and all seemed well. Suddenly we began to talk of the children's education. I do not remember what words either of us said, but a discussion began, with each of us complaining, and with jumps from one subject to another.

"'Yes, I know it. It has been so for a long time...'

" 'You said that. . . .'

"'No, I did not say that. . . .

"'Then I lie?' and so on.

"I felt that the terrible time was approaching when I should want to kill her or else myself. I knew that it was approaching; I was afraid of it, as of fire. I wanted to hold myself back, but anger took possession of my whole being.

"My wife found herself in the same condition, perhaps worse. She knew that she changed each of my words on purpose, and each of her words was filled with poison. All that was dear to me she ran down and made terrible. And the longer the quarrel went on, the worse it became.

"I cried, 'Be silent,' or something like that. And she ran out of the room toward the children. I tried to hold her back, to finish the terrible things I was saying. I grasped her by the arm, and hurt her.

"She cried: 'Children, your father is beating me.'

"I cried: 'Don't lie.'

"She continued to speak lies for the simple purpose of angering me more. 'Ah, it is not the first time,' or something of that sort.

"The children rushed to her and tried to quiet her.

"I said to her: 'Don't make believe.'

"She said: 'You look upon everything as make-believe. You would kill a person and say he was making believe. Now I understand you. That is what you want!'

"'Oh, if you were only dead!' I cried.

"I remember how that terrible phrase filled me with fear. Never had I thought that I could speak words so full of hate, and I was shocked at what had just escaped my lips.

"I ran into my study. I sat down and began to smoke. I heard her go into the hall and prepare to go out. I followed her and asked: 'Where are you going?'

"She did not answer.

"'Well, may the devil take you!' said I to myself.

"I went back into my study, where I lay down and began smoking again. Thousands of plans for getting back at her, for getting rid of her and how to arrange it and act as if nothing had happened – all this passed through my head.

"I thought of these things, and I smoked, and smoked, and smoked. I thought of running away, of making my escape, of going to America. I went so far as to dream how beautiful it would be, after getting rid of her, to love another woman, entirely different from her.

"I should be rid of her if she should die or if we should separate, and I tried to think how that could be managed. I saw that I was getting mixed up but, in order not to see that I was not thinking rightly, I kept on smoking.

"The life of the house went on as usual. The children's teacher came and asked: 'Where is Madame? When will she return?' The help asked if they should serve the tea.

"I entered the dining-room. The children were there. Lise, the eldest girl, looked at me with fear, as if to question me. But their mother did not come. The whole evening passed, and still she did not come.

"Two feelings kept succeeding each other in me, hate for her since she pained me and the children by being absent, but would finally return just the same, and fear that she might return and make some attempt upon herself.

"But where should I look for her? At her sister's? I would be shamed to go there to ask where my wife is. At the same time, I hoped she should be at her sister's! If she wishes to pain any one, let her pain herself first.

"But suppose she were not at her sister's. Suppose she were to do, or had already done, something?

"Eleven o'clock, midnight, one o'clock. . . . I did not sleep. I did not go to my room. It is terrible to lie stretched out all alone, and to wait. But in my study I did not rest. I tried to busy myself, to write letters, to read.

"Impossible! I was alone, in pain, and, thinking evil, I listened. Toward day-light I went to sleep.

"I woke. She had not returned.

"Everything in the house went on as usual, and all looked at me in surprise, with questioning eyes. The children's eyes were full of blame for me.

"And always the same feeling of anxiety about her, and of hate because of this anxiety.

"Toward eleven o'clock in the morning came her sister, concerned. Then began the usual phrases:

"'She is in a terrible state. What is the matter?'

"'Why, nothing has happened.'

"I spoke of her sister's sharp character, and added that I had done nothing, and would not take the first step.

"'If she wants us to part, so much the better!'

"My sister-in-law would not listen to this idea, and went away without having gained anything.

"As soon as she left, I went into the other room and saw the children in a fearful state. There I found myself already willing to take this first step.

"But I was bound by my word. Again I walked up and down, always smoking.

"At breakfast I drank wine, and I reached the point I had not known I desired, where I no longer saw how crazy and base my situation was.

"Toward three o'clock she came. I thought her feelings had eased, or she admitted her defeat. I began to tell her that I was angered by what she had said to me.

"She answered me with a stiff, sour face that she had not come for me to explain things, but to take the children, that we could not live together. I answered that it was not my fault, that she had put me beside myself.

"She looked at me with a quiet, bitter air, and said: 'Say no more. You will be sorry.'

"I said that I could not put up with her play-acting.

"Then she cried something I did not understand, and rushed toward her room. The key turned in the lock, and she shut herself up.

"I pushed at the door. There was no answer. In a fury, I went away.

"A half hour later Lise came running in, all in tears. What! Has anything happened?

"'We cannot hear Mamma!'

"We went to my wife's room. I pushed the door with all my might. The lock was scarcely drawn, and the door opened. My wife, in a skirt, with high shoes, lay on the bed. On the table there was an empty medicine bottle.

"We brought her back to life. Tears and then peace, love! Not peace, really; inside, each kept the hate for the other, but it was absolutely necessary for the moment to end the scene in some way, and life began again as before.

"These scenes, and even worse, came now once a week, now every month, now every day. And always the same.

"Once, I had made up my mind to flee, but through some weakness I didn't understand, I stayed.

"Such were the circumstances in which we were living when the MAN came. The man was bad, it is true. But no worse than we were."

CHAPTER XXI

"When we moved to Moscow, this gentleman – his name was Troukhatchevsky – came to my house.

"It was in the morning. I received him. In former times we had been very familiar. He tried, by various advances, to establish again the familiarity we had once had, but I was determined to keep him at a distance, and soon he gave it up.

"I did not like him at all. At the first glance I saw that he was a dirty ladies man. I did not trust him, even before he had seen my wife. But some strange power kept me from sending him away, and I suffered his approach.

"What could have been simpler than to talk with him a few minutes, then send him coldly away without introducing him to my wife? But no, as if on purpose, I turned the conversation upon his skill playing the violin, and he answered that he now played the violin more than formerly. He remembered that I used to play.

"I answered that I had given up music, but that my wife played very well.

"Odd thing! Why, in the important events of our life, in those in which a man's fate is decided – as mine was decided in that moment – why in these events is there neither a past nor a future?

"My relations with Troukhatchevsky the first day, at the first hour, were such as they might still have been after all that has happened. I knew that something terrible must result from the presence of this man, and still I could not help being pleasant to him. I introduced him to my wife.

"She was pleased with him. In the beginning, I suppose, because of the pleasure of the violin playing, which she loved. She had even hired for that purpose a violin player from the theatre. But when she glanced at me, she understood my feelings, and hid her impression.

"Then began the game of falsity we both played. I smiled pleasantly, making believe that all this pleased me extremely. He, looking at my wife as all such men look at beautiful women, with an air of being interested solely in the subject of conversation – that is, in that which did not interest him at all.

"She tried to act as if she did not notice. But my expression, my lack of trust, or false smile, which she knew so well, and the glances of the musician, it was plain, excited her. I saw that, after the first interview, her eyes were already shining, shining strangely. Thanks to my lack of trust, between him and her had been immediately established that sort of electric current which is caused by an expression in the smile and in the eyes.

"We talked, at the first interview, of music, of Paris, and of all sorts of ordinary things. He rose to go. Pressing his hat against his body, he stood erect, looking now at her and now at me, as if waiting to see what she would do.

"I remember that minute, especially because it was in my power not to invite him. I need not have invited him, and then nothing would have happened. But I glanced first at him, then at her. 'Don't flatter yourself that I can be made uneasy by you,' I thought, addressing myself to her mentally, and I invited the other to bring his violin that very evening, and to play with my wife.

"She turned purple, as if she were seized with a sudden fear. She began to excuse herself, saying that she did not play well enough. This only excited me the more. I remember the strange feeling with which I looked at the man's neck, his white neck, and at his black hair.

"I could not help knowing that this man's presence caused me suffering. 'It is in my power,' thought I, 'to so arrange things that I shall never see him again. But can it be that I fear him? No, I do not fear him. It would be too base of me!' And there in the hall, knowing that my wife heard me, I insisted he come that very evening with his violin.

"He promised me, and went away.

"In the evening he arrived with his violin, and they played together. But for a long time things did not go well. We had not the necessary music, and that which we had my wife could not play at sight.

"I busied myself with their difficulties. I helped them, I made proposals, and they finally played a few pieces – songs without words, some Schubert, and a little piece by Mozart.

"As for difficulties, there were none for him. Scarcely had he begun to play, when his face changed. He became serious, and filled with sympathy.

"He was, it is needless to say, much better than my wife. He helped her, he gave her advice, simply and naturally, and at the same time played his game with good manners.

"My wife seemed interested only in the music. She was very simple and pleasant. Throughout the evening I pretended, not only for the others, but for myself, an interest only in the music. But I continued to be pained.

"From the first minute the musician's eyes met those of my wife, I saw that he did not regard her as a woman without charm, but one with whom on occasion it might be pleasant to enter into closer relations.

"If I had been pure, I should not have dreamed of what he might think of her. But I looked at women the same way, and that is why I understood him and was in pain. I was in pain, especially, because I was sure that toward me she had no other feeling than of always being angry, sometimes interrupted by physical desire.

"But I also knew that this man – thanks to his appearance and the fact that he was new, and, above all, thanks to his great talent, to the appeal he made under the influence of music, and to the impression that music produces upon nervous natures – that this man would not only please, but would, without difficulty, be able to do with her as he liked.

"I could not help seeing this. I could not help suffering. And perhaps even because of that, some force made me be not only polite, but more than polite, friendly.

"I cannot say whether I did it for my wife, or to show him I did not fear HIM, or did it to fool myself; but from my first relations with him I could not but make believe I was at my ease.

"I was forced, that I might not give way to a desire to kill him immediately.

To be especially friendly him, I filled his glass at the table, I praised his playing, I talked to him with a pleasant smile, and I invited him to dinner the following Sunday to play again. I told him that I would invite some of my friends, lovers of his art, to hear him.

"Two or three days later I was entering my house in conversation with a friend, when in the hall I suddenly felt something heavy, like a stone, weighing on my heart. I could not account for it.

"It was this: in passing through the hall, I had noticed something which reminded me of HIM. But it was not until I reached my study did I realize what it was.

"I returned to the hall to make sure I was not mistaken. Yes, I was not mistaken. It was his coat. I questioned the help. That was it. He had come.

"I passed near the living-room, through the children's study. Lise, my daughter, was sitting before a book, and the old nurse, with my youngest child, was beside the table, turning the cover of something or other.

"In the living-room I heard a slow movement being played on the piano, and his voice, very quiet, saying something to her, and her denying it.

"She said: 'No, no! There is something else!'

"It seemed to me that some one was covering the words with the aid of the piano. My God! How my heart jumped! What didn't I imagine!

"When I remember the beast that lived in me at that moment, I am seized by fear. My heart was first seized tightly, then stopped, and began to beat loudly. The main feeling I had, as in every bad feeling, was pity for myself.

'Before the children, before the old nurse,' thought I, 'she shames me. I will go away. I can endure it no longer. God knows what I should do if. . . . But I must go in.'

"The old nurse raised her eyes to mine, as if she understood, and advised me to keep a sharp watch.

"Without knowing what I did, I opened the door. He was sitting at the piano playing with his long, white, curved fingers. She was standing in the angle of the grand piano, before the open score.

"She saw or heard me first, and raised her eyes to mine. Was she shocked, was she making believe she had no fear, or did she really have no fear? In any case, she did not tremble, she did not stir. She turned red, but only later.

"'How glad I am that you have come! We have not decided what we will play Sunday,' said she, in a tone she would not have had if she had been alone with me.

"This tone, and the way in which she said 'we' in speaking of herself and of him, turned my stomach. I nodded silently to him. He shook hands with me with a smile that seemed false. He explained to me that he had brought some scores in order to prepare for the Sunday concert, and that they were not in agreement as to the piece to choose – whether something difficult and well-known, something by Beethoven, say, or lighter pieces.

"As he spoke, he looked at me. It was all so natural, so simple, that there was absolutely nothing to be said against it. At the same time I saw, I was sure, that it was false, that they were, together, trying to fool me.

"One of the most painful situations for those who are without trust (and in our social life everybody is without trust) are those social conditions which allow a very great and dangerous closeness between a man and a woman in certain circumstances.

"One must make himself the laughing stock of everybody if he desires to prevent associations in the ball-room, the closeness of doctors with their patients, the familiarity that art occasions, and especially music.

"In order that people may occupy themselves together with the noblest art – music – certain closeness is necessary in which there is nothing wrong.

"Only a fool of a husband, who does not trust his wife, can have anything to say against it. A husband should not have such thoughts, and especially should not stick his nose into these affairs, or try to stop them.

"And yet, everybody knows that it is in these occupations, especially in music, that many of the sins in our society begin.

"I must have interrupted them, because for some time I couldn't say anything. I was like a bottle, suddenly turned upside down, from which the water does not run because it is too full. I was angry and wanted to drive the man away, but I could do nothing of the kind.

"Instead, I felt I that I was in the way, and that it was my fault. I made believe that I thought everything was fine – this time, also, thanks to that feeling that forced me to treat him the more pleasantly the more his being there was painful to me.

"I said that I trusted to his taste, and I told my wife to do the same. He stayed just as long as it was necessary to rid us of the bad impression I had made on my entrance. He went away with a satisfied air.

"As for me, I was perfectly sure that, in that which truly concerned them, the question of music was the least important.

"I was very pleasant as I accompanied him to the hall (how can one help accompanying a man who has come to disturb your peace and ruin the happiness of the entire family?), and I shook his white, soft hand with extra friendliness."

CHAPTER XXII

"All that day I did not speak to my wife. I could not. Her nearness excited such hatred that I feared myself.

"At the table she asked me, in the presence of the children, when I was to start upon a journey. I was to go the following week to an assembly of the Zemstvo in a neighboring locality. I named the date.

"She asked me if I would need anything for the journey. I did not answer. I sat silent at the table, and silently I retired to my study. In those last days she never entered my study, especially at that hour.

"Suddenly I heard her steps, her walk, and then a terribly base idea entered my head that, like the wife of Uri, she wished to hide a sin already done, and that it was for this reason that she came to see me at this hour.

"As she approached, I thought: 'If it is to see me that she is coming, then I am right.'

"A terrible hate came into my head.

"The steps drew nearer, and nearer yet. Would she pass by and go on to the other room? No, the door made a noise, and her tall, graceful figure appeared.

"In her face, in her eyes, there was a shyness mixed with fear, an expression she tried to hide, but which I saw, and of which I understood the meaning. I came near losing my senses, such were my efforts to hold my breath, and, continuing to look at her, I took my cigarette, and lighted it.

"'What does this mean? One comes to talk with you, and you go to smoking.'

"She sat down beside me on the sofa, resting against my shoulder. I pulled away, that I might not touch her.

"'I see that you are not pleased with what I wish to play on Sunday,' said she.

"'That is not true,' said I.

"'Can I not see?'

"'Well, I praise your ability to see. Only, to you everything base is pleasant, and I hate it like hell.'

"'If you are going to swear like a trooper, I am going away.'

"'Then go away. Only know that, if the honor of the family is nothing to you, to me it is dear. As for you, the devil take you!'

"'What! What is the matter?'

"'Go away, in the name of God.'

"But she did not go away. Was she making believe she did not understand, or did she really not understand what I meant? But she was hurt and became angry.

"'You have become absolutely impossible,' she began, or some such phrase as that regarding my character, trying, as usual, to give me as much pain as possible.

"'After what you have done to my sister (she was talking about a time when, beside myself, I had said some terrible things to her sister; she knew that that shamed me, and tried to touch me in that tender spot) nothing will astonish me.'

"'Yes, pained, made to feel base, and shamed, and after that to hold me still responsible,' thought I, and suddenly a rage, a hate, came over me I do not remember ever having felt before.

"For the first time I desired to express this hate physically. I jumped on her, but at the same moment I understood how I was feeling, and I asked myself whether it would be well for me to give myself up to my fury.

"I answered myself that it would be well, that it would make her fear me, and, instead of holding myself back, I egged myself on. I was glad to feel my anger boiling, making me more and more fierce.

"'Go away, or I will kill you!' I cried with a loud voice, and I grasped her by the arm. She did not go away. Then I turned her arm, and roughly pushed her away.

"'What is the matter with you? Come to your senses!' she cried.

"'Go away,' roared I, louder than ever, rolling my eyes wildly. 'It takes you to put me in such a fury. I do not answer for myself! Go away!'

"In giving myself to my anger, I became filled with it, and I wanted to do something to show the force of my fury. I felt a terrible desire to beat her, to kill her, but I realized that that could not be, and I held myself back. I drew away from her, rushed to the table, grasped the paper-weight, and threw it on the floor by her side. I took care to aim a little to one side, and, before she disappeared (I did it so that she could see it), I grasped a book, which I also threw, and then picked up a fire iron, continuing to shout:

"'Go away! I do not answer for myself!'

"She disappeared, and I immediately stopped my acting out. An hour later the old servant came to me and said that my wife was in a fit. I went to see her. She cried and laughed, not able to speak, her whole body in a tremble. She was not making believe, she was really sick. We sent for the doctor, and all night long I cared for her.

"Toward dawn she grew calmer, and we made up under the influence of that feeling we called 'love.' The next morning, after we had made peace, I told her that I did not trust Troukhatchevsky. She was not at all shamed, and began to laugh in the most natural way, so strange did the possibility of being led to sin by such a man appear to her.

"'With such a man can an honest woman have any feeling beyond the pleasure of enjoying music with him? But if you like, I am ready to never see him again, even on Sunday, although everybody has been invited. Write him that I am not well, and that will end the matter. Only there is one thing I do not like – that any one could have thought him dangerous. I am too proud not to hate such thoughts.'

"And she did not lie. She believed what she said. She hoped by her words to make herself feel that he was beneath her, and thus to defend herself. But she did not succeed. Everything was against her, especially that terrible music. So ended the quarrel, and on Sunday our guests came, and Troukhatchevsky and my wife again played together."

Chapter XXIII

"I don't think it's too much to say I was very vain. If one has no pride of self in this life of ours, there is not enough reason for living. So, for that Sunday I arranged for the dinner and the music to follow, so that everything would be in good taste. And I chose the guests myself.

"Toward six o'clock they arrived, and after them Troukhatchevsky, in his dress-coat, with diamond shirt-studs that were in such bad taste! But he bore himself with ease. To all questions he responded promptly, with a smile of contentment and understanding, and that peculiar expression which was intended to mean: 'All that you may do and say will be exactly what I expected.'

"Everything about him that was not correct I now noticed with special pleasure, for it all tended to put me at ease, and prove to me that he stood in such a degree of inferiority that, as my wife had told me, she could not stoop to his level. And, less because of my wife's assurances than because of the pain, I no longer allowed myself to be without trust.

"And yet I was not at ease with the musician or with her during dinner-time and the time that passed before the beginning of the music. I couldn't help following each of their gestures and looks.

"Not long after a boring dinner, the music began. He went to get his violin; my wife advanced to the piano, and searched among the scores.

"Oh, how well I remember all the details of that evening! I remember how he brought the violin, how he opened the box, took the cloth

81

covering from the violin, and began to get the instrument ready to play.

"I can still see my wife sit down, with a false air of being above it all. But it was plain she hid a great state of nerves, nerves that were especially due to her lack of musical knowledge compared to his.

"She sat down with that false air in front of the piano, and then began the usual preliminaries – the picking of the strings of the violin and the arrangement of the scores. I remember then how they looked at each other, and cast a glance at the guests, who were taking their seats.

"They said a few words to each other, and the music began. They played Beethoven's 'Kreutzer Sonata.' Do you know the lively beginning? Do you know it? Ah!" . . .

Posdnicheff heaved a sigh, and was silent for a long time.

"A terrible thing is that music, especially the lively beginning! And a terrible thing is music in general. What is it? Why does it do what it does? They say that music stirs the soul. A lie! It acts, it acts fearfully (I speak for myself), but not in a way that makes one feel noble or base.

"How shall I say it? Music makes me forget my real situation. It puts me into a state which is not my own. Under the influence of music I really seem to feel what I do not feel, to understand what I do not understand, to have powers which I cannot have.

"Music seems to me like laughter; I have no desire to laugh, but I laugh when I hear others laugh. And music immediately put me into the condition in which he who wrote the music found himself at that time.

"My feelings and thoughts become mixed with his, and with him I pass from one condition to another. But why that? I know nothing about it? But Beethoven, who wrote the 'Kreutzer Sonata', knew well why he found himself in a certain condition. That condition led him to certain actions, and for that reason to him the music had a meaning, but to me none, none whatever. And that is why music makes us excited, but does not bring us to an end.

"For instance, a military march is played; the soldier passes to the sound of this march, and the music is finished. A dance is played; I have finished dancing, and the music is finished. A mass is sung; I receive the sacrament, and again the music is finished. Any other music makes us excited, and it is not accompanied by the thing that needs properly to be done, and that is why music is so dangerous, and sometimes acts so fearfully.

"In China music is under the control of the State, and that is the way it ought to be. Is it right that the first comer should put one or more persons under his spell, and then do with them as he likes? And especially that he who does that should be the first immoral individual who happens to come along?

"It is a frightful power in the hands of any one, no matter who it is. For instance, should they be allowed to play this 'Kreutzer Sonata,' and there are many like It, in rooms, among ladies wearing low necked dresses, or in concerts, then finish the piece, receive the applause, and then begin another piece?

"These things should be played under certain circumstances, only in cases where it is necessary to encourage certain actions in line with the music. But to stir up an energy of feeling which matches neither the time nor the place, and is spent in nothing, cannot fail to act dangerously.

"On me in particular this piece acted in a fearful manner. One would have said that new feelings, new realities, of which I formerly did not know, had developed In me. 'Ah, yes, that's it! Not at all as I lived and thought before! This is the right way to live!'

"Thus I spoke to myself as I listened to that music. What was this new thing that I thus learned? *That* I did not realize, but just being in this state filled me with joy. In that state there was no room for lack of trust.

"The same faces, and among them HE and my wife, I saw in a different light. This music took me into a world I was not used to, where there was no room for lack of trust. Lack of trust and the feelings that cause it seemed to me small things, nor worth thinking of.

"After the lively opening followed the slower movement, not very new, with ordinary changes, and the weak ending. Then they played more, at the request of the guests – first a sad piece by Ernst, and then various other pieces. They were all very well, but did not produce upon me a tenth part of the impression that the opening piece did.

"I felt light and gay through all the evening. As for my wife, never had I seen her as she was that night. Those bright eyes, that serious and noble expression while she was playing, and then that utter tiredness, that weak and happy smile after she had finished – I saw them all and gave no importance to them, believing that she felt as I did, that to her, as to me, new feelings had been revealed.

"During almost the whole evening I had no lack of trust.

"Two days later I was to start for the meeting of the Zemstvo, and for that reason, on taking leave of me and carrying all his scores with him, Troukhatchevsky asked me when I should return. I understood from that that he believed it impossible to come to my house when I was absent, and that was fine with me.

"Now, I was not to return before he left the city. So we said good-bye to each other. For the first time I shook his hand with pleasure, and thanked him for the satisfaction that he had given me. He likewise took leave of my wife, and their parting seemed to me very natural and proper.

"All went very well. My wife and I went to bed, well satisfied with the evening. We talked of our impressions in a general way, and we were nearer together and more friendly than we had been for a long time."

Chapter XXIV

"Two days later I started for the meeting of the Zemstvo, having said good-bye to my wife in an excellent and peaceful state of mind.

"In the district there was always much to be done. It was a world and a life apart. During two days I spent ten hours at the meetings. The evening of the second day, on returning to my room, I found a letter from my wife, telling me of the children, of their uncle, of the help, and, among other things, as if it were perfectly natural, that Troukhatchevsky had been at the house, and had brought her the promised scores. He had also proposed that they play again, but she had refused.

"For my part, I did not remember at all that he had promised any score. It had seemed to me on Sunday evening that he took an absolute leave, and for this reason the news gave me an uneasy surprise.

"I read the letter again. There was something tender about it. It produced an extremely painful impression upon me. My heart swelled, and the mad, jealous beast that I was began to roar. It wanted to spring, but I was afraid of this beast, and I made it be quiet.

"How I hate this feeling of not trusting! 'What could be more natural than what she has written?' said I to myself. I went to bed, thinking myself at peace again. I thought of the business that still must be done, and I went to sleep without thinking of her.

"During these meetings of the Zemstvo I always slept badly in my strange quarters. That night I went to sleep directly, but, as sometimes happens, a sort of sudden shock awoke me.

"I thought immediately of her, of my physical love for her, of Troukhatchevsky, and that between them everything had happened. And a feeling of great anger tightened my heart. I tried to quiet myself.

"'How foolish!' said I to myself; 'there is no reason, none at all. And why do ourselves harm, herself and myself, and especially myself, by supposing such a thing?

"This musician, known as a bad man – shall I think of him in connection with a respectable woman, the mother of a family, MY wife? How foolish!' But on the other hand, I said to myself: 'Why should it not happen?'

"Why? Was it not the same simple, understandable feeling in the name of which I married, in the name of which I was living with her, the only thing I wanted of her, and that which, naturally, others desired, this musician among the rest?

"He was not married, was in good health (I remember how his teeth ground the meat of the dinner, and how eagerly he emptied the glass of wine with his red lips), was careful of his person, well fed, and not only without principles, but evidently with the principle that one should take advantage of the pleasure that offers itself.

"There was a bond between them, music – the most advanced form of pleasure. What was there to hold them back? Nothing.

"Everything, on the other hand, drew them to each other. And she, she had been and was a mystery. I did not know her. I knew her only as an animal, and an animal nothing could or should hold back.

"And now I remember their faces on Sunday evening, when, after the 'Kreutzer Sonata,' they played a piece, written I know not by whom, but with so much passion it could be called a sin.

"'How could I have gone away?' said I to myself, as I remembered their faces. 'Was it not clear that between them everything was done that evening? Was it not clear that between them not only was there nothing to keep them from going further, but that both – specially she – felt a certain shame after what had happened at the piano?

"How weakly, but happily, she smiled, as she wiped the drops from her face made red by her effort! They already avoided each other's eyes, and only at the supper, when she poured some water for him, did they look at each other and smile, a smile that was hardly noticeable.'

"Now I remember with fear that look and that scarcely seen smile. 'Yes, everything has happened,' a voice said to me, and directly another said the opposite. 'Are you mad? It is impossible!' said the second voice.

"It was too painful to me to remain thus stretched in the darkness. I struck a match, and the little yellow-papered room filled me with fear. I lit a cigarette, and, as always happens when one is in such a state, I began to smoke.

"I smoked cigarette after cigarette to dull my senses, that I might not see or feel all that was going on.

"All night I did not sleep, and at five o'clock, when it was not yet light, I decided I could stand the strain no longer, and that I would leave directly. There was a train at eight o'clock.

"I woke the keeper who was acting as my help, and sent him to look for horses. To the meeting of Zemstvo I sent a message that I was called back to Moscow by pressing business, and begged them to name another as a member of the Committee.

"A few minutes after that I got into a wagon and started off."

CHAPTER XXV

"I had to go twenty-five miles by wagon and eight hours by train. By wagon it was a very pleasant journey.

"The coolness of autumn was accompanied by a bright sun. You know the weather when the wheels leave a mark on the road. The road was level, the light strong, and the air strengthening. The wagon was comfortable.

As I looked at the horses, the fields, and the people whom we passed, I forgot where I was going. Sometimes it seemed to me that I was travelling without an object, and that I should go on thus to the end of the world.

"I was happy when I so forgot myself. But when I remembered where I was going, I said to myself: 'I shall see later. Don't think about it.'

"When we were half way home, an accident happened that took take my thoughts still further away. The wagon, though new, broke down, and had to be repaired.

"The delays in looking for a part, the repairs, the payment, the tea in the inn, the conversation with the owner, all served to keep my mind occupied. Toward night-fall all was ready, and I started off again.

"By night the journey was still pleasanter than by day. The moon in its first quarter, a slight bit of ice on the grass, the road still in good condition, the horses, the happy driver, all served to put me in good spirits.

"I scarcely thought of what waited me for me ahead, and was happy perhaps because of the very thing that was waiting for me, and because I was about to say good-bye to the joys of life.

"But this peaceful state, the power of putting aside what was making me feel bad, ended with the wagon drive. Scarcely had I entered the train, when the other thing began. Those eight hours on the rail were so terrible to me that I shall never forget them in my life.

"Was it because on entering the train I imagined I had already arrived, or because the railway acts upon people in such a fashion?

"At any rate, after boarding the train I could no longer control my imagining. My mind kept drawing pictures before my eyes, each worse than the one before.

"That increased my jealousy. And always it was the same things, about what was happening at home while I was absent. I burned with rage, and with a strange feeling that I had been made a fool of.

"I could not tear myself out of this condition. I could not help looking at the pictures in my head. I could not make them go away, I could not keep from imagining them. And the more I looked at them, the more I believed in their reality, forgetting that they had no serious foundation.

"The strength of these images seemed to prove to me that they were a reality.

"One would have said that a devil, against my will, was making them up and breathing life into them.

"A conversation, dating a long time back, that I had had with the brother of Troukhatchevsky, I remembered at that moment. It took place a long time ago, but it tore my heart as I connected it with the musician and my wife.

"The brother of Troukhatchevsky, in answering my question as to whether he frequented houses of ill-fame, said that a respectable man does not go where he may contract a disease, when one can find an honest woman.

"And here he, his brother, the musician, had found the honest woman!

"'It is true that she is no longer in her early youth. She has lost a tooth on one side, and her face is slightly bloated,' thought I for

Troukhatchevsky. 'But what is to be done? One must profit by what one has.'

"'Yes, he is bound to take her for his mistress,' said I to myself again; 'and besides, she is not dangerous.'

"'No, it is not possible' I said in fear. 'Nothing, nothing of the kind has happened, and there is no reason to suppose there has. Did she not tell me that the very idea that I could lack trust in her because of him shamed her?'

'Yes, but she lied,' I cried, and everything began all over again.

"There were only two travelers in my part of the train: an old woman with her husband, neither of whom said very much; and even they got out at one of the stations, leaving me all alone.

"I was like a beast in a cage. Now I jumped up and approached the window, now I began to walk back and forth, pushing forward as if I hoped to make the train go faster, and the car with its seats and its windows continued to tremble, as ours does now."

Posdnicheff rose suddenly, took a few steps, and sat down again.

"Oh, I am afraid of railway trains," he said. "Fear seized me. I sat down again, and I said to myself: 'I must think of something else. For instance, think of the inn keeper at whose house I took tea.'

"And then, in my imagining I saw the picture of him with his long beard, and his grandson, a little fellow of the same age as my little Basile.

"My little Basile! My little Basile! He will see the musician kiss his mother! What thoughts will pass through his head! But what does that matter to her! She loves the musician.

"And again it all began, the circle of the same thoughts.

"I suffered so much that at last I did not know what to do with myself, and an idea passed through my head that pleased me much – to get out upon the rails, throw myself under the cars, and thus finish everything.

"One thing prevented me from doing so. It was pity! It was pity for myself, bringing up at the same time hate for her, for him, but not so much for him.

"Toward him I felt a strange feeling of my shame for his victory, but toward her I felt a terrible hate.

"'But I cannot kill myself and leave her free. She must suffer, she must understand at least that I have suffered,' said I to myself.

"At a station I saw people drinking at the lunch counter, and directly I went to have a drink. Beside me stood a laborer drinking also. He began to talk to me, and I, in order not to be left alone in my part of the train, went with him into his third-class car, which was dirty, full of smoke, and covered with fruit skins and sun-flower seeds.

"There I sat down beside him, and, as it seemed, he told many stories. First I listened to him, but I did not understand what he said. I rose and entered my own car.

"'I must consider,' said I to myself, 'whether what I think is true, whether there is any reason for me to suspect anything.' I sat down, wishing to think quietly; but directly, instead of peaceful thoughts, the same thing began again. Instead of reasoning, the pictures in my head began again.

"'How many times have I given myself pain in this way,' I thought (I remembered previous and similar fits of jealousy), 'and then seen it end in nothing at all?

"It is the same now. Perhaps I shall find her quietly sleeping. She will waken, she will be glad, and in her words and looks I shall see that nothing has happened, that all this is vain.

"'Ah, if it would only turn out so!'

"'But no, that has happened too often! Now the end has come,' a voice said to me. And again it all began.

"Ah, what pain! It is not to a hospital filled with patients suffering from the diseases of love that I would take a young man to deprive him of the desire for women, but into my mind, to show him the devil tearing it apart.

"The worst part was that I recognized in myself a right to the body of my wife, as if her body were entirely mine. At the same time I felt that I could not possess this body, that it was not mine, that she could do with it as she liked.

"But she liked to do with it as I did not like. And I was powerless against him and against her.

"He, like the Vanka of the song, would sing, before mounting the gallows, how he would kiss her sweet lips, and so on, and he would even have the best of it before death. With her it was still worse.

"If she HAD NOT DONE IT, she had the desire, she wished to do it, and I knew that she did. That was worse. It were better if she had already done it, to give me relief from my doubt. In short, I could not say what I desired. I desired that she might not want what she MUST want. It was complete madness."

Chapter XXVI

"At the next to last station, when the conductor came to take the tickets, I took my bags and went out on the car platform.

"Knowing that the end was near only added to my anxiety. I was cold, my jaw trembled so that my teeth knocked together.

"Without thinking, I left the station with the crowd and got a ride. I looked at the few people passing in the streets. I read the signs without thinking of anything.

"After half a mile my feet began to feel cold, and I remembered that in the car I had taken off my wool socks, and had put them in my travelling bag. Where had I put the bag? Was it with me? Yes, and the basket?

"I thought I had totally forgotten my bags. I took out my check for them, but then decided it was not worth my while to return for them, and continued on my way.

"After all my efforts to remember, I cannot at this moment make out why I was in such a hurry. I knew only that a serious and fearful event was approaching in my life.

"It was a case of self-suggestion.

"Was it so serious because I thought it so? Or was it just a sense I had? I do not know. Perhaps after what has happened, all previous events have taken on a black coloring.

"When I arrived at the steps, it was an hour past midnight. There were a few wagons before the door waiting for possible riders. They were probably attracted by the lighted windows (the lighted windows were those of our living room and entrance).

"Without trying to account for these late lights, I went up the steps, still expecting something terrible, and rang the bell.

"A good, hard-working, but very stupid being, named Gregor, opened the door. The first thing saw in the hall, on the hat-stand, among other clothes, was an over-coat. I ought to have been surprised, but I was not. I expected it. 'That's it!' I said to myself.

"When I asked Gregor who was there, and he named Troukhatchevsky, I asked whether there were other visitors.

"He answered: 'Nobody.'

"I remember the air with which he said that, as if he intended to give me pleasure, and dissipate my doubts.

"'That's it! That's it!' I said to myself.

"'And the children?' I asked.

"'They went to sleep long ago.'

"'Thank God, they are well,' I thought.

"I scarcely breathed, and I could not keep my lips from trembling. Then it was not as I thought. I had often before returned home with the thought that something terrible was waiting me, but had been mistaken, and everything was going on as usual.

"But now things were not going on as usual. All that I had imagined, all that I believed to be dreams, all really existed. Here was the truth.

"I was on the point of weeping, but at once the devil whispered in my ear: 'Weep and be all emotion, and they will separate quietly, and you will not be able to prove anything, and all your life you will be in doubt and suffer.'

"Pity for myself left me, and there was only the animal-like need for some careful, thought-out, energetic action. I became a beast, a thoughtful beast.

"'No, no,' said I to Gregor, who was about to announce my arrival. 'Do this instead. Take a wagon and go at once for my bags. Here is the check. Go now.'

"He went along the hall to get his over-coat.

"Fearing he might give me away, I accompanied him to his little room, and waited for him to put on his things.

"In the dining-room could be heard the sound of conversation and the noise of knives and plates. They were eating. They had not heard the ring.

"'Now if they only do not go out,' I thought.

"Gregor put on his fur coat and went out. I closed the door after him. I felt anxious when I was alone, thinking that directly I should have to act. How?

"I did not yet know. I knew only that all was ended, that there could be no doubt of his guilt, and that in an instant my relations with her were going to be brought to an end.

Before, I still had doubts. I said to myself: 'Perhaps this is not true. Perhaps I am mistaken.'

"Now all doubt had disappeared. All was decided.

"Secretly, all alone with him, at night! It is breaking all the rules! Or, worse yet, she may make a show, put up a front of being without guilt, which, when there has been a crime, by its excess tends to prove the opposite.

"All is clear. No doubt about it

"I feared but one thing now, that they might run in different directions, that they might invent some new lie, and thus take from me the material proof of their guilt, and the sad joy of punishing, yes, of killing them.

"To surprise them more quickly, I started on tip-toe for the dining-room, not through the living room, but through the hall and the children's rooms.

"In the first room slept the little boy. In the second, the old nurse moved in her bed, and seemed on the point of waking. I wondered what she would think when she knew all. Pity for myself gave me such a hurt feeling that I could not keep the tears back.

"Not to wake the children, I ran lightly through the hall into my study. I dropped upon the sofa, and wept.

"'I, an honest man, I, the son of my parents, who all my life long have dreamed of family happiness, I who have never done anything to destroy her trust . . . this is happening to me! And here are my five children, and she kissing a musician because he has red lips!

"No, she is not a woman! She is an animal, a dirty animal! And doing it next to the children's room, whom she had pretended to love all her life!

"Then to think of what she wrote me! And how do I know? Perhaps it has always been thus. Perhaps all these children, supposed to be mine, are the children of others.

"If I had arrived tomorrow, she would have come to meet me with her hair all done up, carrying flowers, with her slow, beautiful movements (and I see her good-looking but base features), and this evil animal would have remained forever in my heart, tearing it apart.

"What will the old nurse say? And Gregor? And poor little Lise? She already understands things. And this nerve, this falsity, this animal-like desire I know so well,' I said to myself.

"I tried to rise, but could not. My heart was beating so strongly I could not hold myself upon my legs.

"'Yes, I shall die of a rush of blood. She will kill me. That is what she wants. What is it to her to kill?

"But that would be great for him, and I will not allow him to have this pleasure.

"'Yes, here I am, and there they are. They are laughing, they. . . . Yes, in spite of the fact that she is no longer in her early youth, he has not looked away from her.

"At any rate, she is by no means ugly, and above all, not dangerous to his dear health, to him. Why did I not kill her then?' said I, remembering the scene of the other week, when I drove her from my study and broke the furniture.

"I remembered the state I was in. Not only did I remember it, but I again entered into the same animal-like state. And suddenly there came to me a desire to act, and all reasoning, except such as was necessary to action, left my brain.

"I was like a beast, a man excited in the face of danger, but who acts calmly, without haste, and yet without losing a minute, with a single object in mind.

"The first thing that I did was to take off my boots and, in my stockings, advance toward the wall behind the chair where the fire-arms and knives were hanging.

"I took down a curved Damascus sword, which I had never used and which was very sharp. I drew it from its cover, and the cover fell behind the chair.

" I remember saying to myself: 'I must look for it later; it must not be lost.'

"Then I took off my over-coat, which I had kept on all this time, and quietly, with animal-like steps I started for THE ROOM.

"I do not remember how I proceeded, whether I ran, or went slowly, through what rooms I passed, how I approached the dining-room, how I opened the door, how I entered."

Chapter XXVII

"I remember only the expression on their faces when I opened the door. I remember it because it wakened in me a feeling of terrible joy. It was an expression of sudden and desperate fear.

"He, I believe, was at the table, and, when he saw or heard me, he started, jumped to his feet, and retreated to the side-board. Fear was the only feeling that could be read with certainty in his face.

"In hers, too, fear was to be read, but it was accompanied by other impressions. And yet, if her face had expressed only fear, perhaps that which happened would not have happened.

"For in the expression on her face there was at the first moment – at least, I thought I saw it – a feeling of not being pleased at this interruption.

"One would have said that her sole desire was not to be interrupted IN THE MOMENT OF HER HAPPINESS.

"But these expressions appeared upon their faces only for a moment. The fear almost immediately gave place to questioning. Would they lie or not?

"If yes, they must begin. If not, something else was going to happen. But what?

"He gave her a questioning glance.

"On her face the expression of not being pleased at the interruption changed, it seemed to me, when she looked at him, into an expression of anxiety for HIM.

"For a moment I stood in the doorway, holding the dagger hidden behind my back.

"Suddenly he smiled, and in a voice so calm it was as if he was making fun of me, he said:

"'We were having some music.'

"'I did not expect…,' she began at the same time, in the same calm voice.

"But neither he nor she finished their remarks.

"The same rage I had felt the week before took possession of me. I felt the need to give free course to my lack of trust and to 'the joy of wrath.'

"No, they did not finish. That other thing was going to begin, of which he was afraid, and was going to destroy what they wanted to say.

"I threw myself upon her, still hiding the knife that he might not prevent me from striking where I desired – in her bosom, under the breast.

"At that moment he saw . . . and did what I did not expect. He seized my hand and cried: 'Come to your senses! What are you doing? Help! Help!'

"I tore my hands free and leaped upon him.

"I must have been very terrible, for he turned as white as a sheet, to his lips. His eyes had a strange light in them, and again he did what I did not expect of him – he ducked under the piano and ran toward the other room.

"I tried to follow him, but a very heavy weight fell upon my left arm. It was she.

"I made an effort to clear myself.

"She clung more heavily than ever, refusing to let go. This unexpected difficulty, this block, and this unwanted touch only made me more angry.

"I saw that I was completely mad, that I must look fearful, and I was glad of it. Suddenly, with all my strength, I dealt her a blow in the face with my left elbow. She uttered a cry and let go my arm.

"I wanted to follow the other, but I felt that I would look like a fool running after the lover of my wife in my stockings, and I did not wish to appear foolish; I wished to appear terrible.

"In spite of my rage, I was all the time conscious of the impression that I was making upon others, and even this impression partially guided me.

"I turned toward her. She had fallen on the long easy chair. Covering her face where I had struck her, she looked at me. Her eyes were full of fear and hate toward me, her enemy, such as a rat shows when one lifts the rat-trap.

"At least, I saw nothing in her but that fear and hate, the fear and hate which love for another had caused. Perhaps I still should have held myself back, and not have done what I did, if she had maintained silence. But suddenly she began to speak.

"She grasped my hand that held the knife and cried: 'Come to your senses! What are you doing? What is the matter with you? Nothing has happened, nothing, nothing! I swear it to you!'

"I might have delayed longer, but these last words, from which I understood the opposite – that is, that EVERYTHING had happened – these words called for a reply. And the reply must be equal to the condition into which I had gotten myself, and which was increasing and must continue to increase. Rage has its laws.

"'Do not lie, wretch. Do not lie!' I roared.

"With my left hand I seized her hands. She freed herself. Then, without dropping my knife, I seized her by the throat, forced her to the floor, and began to strangle her.

"With her two hands she clutched mine, tearing them from her throat. Then I struck her with the knife, in the left side, between the lower ribs.

"When people say that they do not remember what they do in a fit of fury, they talk nonsense. It is false. I remember everything.

"I did not lose my sense of what I was doing for a single moment. The more I got myself to the fury, the clearer my mind became, and I could not help seeing what I did.

"I cannot say that I knew in advance what I would do, but at the moment when I acted, and it seems to me even a little before, I knew what I was doing.

"It was as if it was to make it possible, later, to say I was sorry, and to be able to say that I could have stopped.

"I knew that I struck the blow between the ribs, and that the knife entered. And at the second when I did it, I knew that I was performing a terrible act, such as I had never performed before, an act that would result in terrible things happening.

"My thought was as quick as lightning, and the deed followed immediately. The act, to my inner sense, had an extraordinary clearness.

"I felt the thickness of the under-clothes and then something else, the sinking of the knife into a soft substance.

"She clutched at the knife with her hands, and cut herself, but she could not keep the blow from happening.

"Long afterward, in prison, when the moral revolution had happened within me, I thought of that minute. I remembered it as far as I could, and made a whole, in my mind, of all the things that had happened.

"I remembered how terrible I felt knowing I was killing a wife, MY wife. Having plunged in the knife, I drew it out again immediately, wishing to stop my action and repair the wounds I had caused.

"She straightened up and cried: 'Nurse, he has killed me!'

"The old nurse, who had heard the noise, was standing in the doorway.

"I was still standing, waiting, not believing myself in what had happened.

"At that moment, from beneath my wife's under-clothes, the blood flowed forth. Then only did I understand that repairing what I had done was impossible.

"I promptly decided that it was not even necessary, that all had happened in accordance with my wish, and that I had fulfilled my desire.

"I waited until she fell, until the nurse, exclaiming, 'Oh, my God!' ran to her; then only I threw away the knife and went out of the room.

"'I must not be excited. I must know what I am doing,' I said to myself, looking neither at my wife nor at the old nurse.

"The latter cried and called the maid.

"I passed through the hall, and, after having sent the maid, started for my study.

"'What shall I do now?' I asked myself.

"Immediately I understood what I should do.

"After entering the study, I went straight to the wall, took down the gun, and examined it carefully.

"It was loaded. I placed it on the table. Next I picked up the cover for the knife, which had dropped behind the chair, and put it back on the wall.

"I then sat down, and remained thus for a long time. I thought of nothing, I did not try to remember anything.

"I heard steps, the movement of objects and drawing of curtains, then the arrival of a person, and then the arrival of another person.

"Then I saw Gregor bring into my room the bags from the railway; as if any one needed them!

"'Have you heard what has happened?' I asked him. 'Have you told the driver to inform the police?'

"He made no answer, and went out. I rose, closed the door, took the cigarettes and the matches, and began to smoke. I had not finished one cigarette, when a sleepy feeling came over me and sent me into a deep sleep.

"I surely slept two hours. I remember having dreamed that I was on good terms with her, that after a quarrel we were in the act of making up, that something prevented us, but that we were friends all the same.

"A knock at the door woke me.

"'It is the police,' thought I as I opened my eyes. 'I have killed her, I believe. But perhaps it is SHE; perhaps nothing has happened.'

"Another knock. I did not answer. I was solving the question: 'Has it happened or not? Yes, it has happened.'

"I remembered the thickness of the under-clothes, and then. . . 'Yes, it has happened. Yes, it has happened. Yes, now I must kill myself,' said I to myself.

"I said it, but I knew very well I would not kill myself. Nevertheless, I rose and took the gun, but, strange thing, I remembered that formerly I had very often had ideas of killing myself, that that very night, on the train, it had seemed to me easy, especially easy because I thought how it would shock her.

"Now I not only could not kill myself, but I could not even think of it.

"'Why do it?' I asked myself, without answering.

"Another knock at the door.

"'Yes, but I must first know who is knocking. I have time enough.'

"I put the gun back on the table, and hid it under my newspaper. I went to the door and drew back the lock.

"It was my wife's sister – a good and stupid widow.

"'Basile, what does this mean?' said she, and her tears, always ready, began to flow.

"'What do you want?' I asked roughly.

"I saw clearly that there was no necessity of being rough with her, but I could not speak in any other tone.

"'Basile, she is dying. Ivan Fedorowitch says so.'

"Ivan Fedorowitch was the doctor, HER doctor, who gave her advice.

"'Is he here?' I asked."And all my hate for her rose again. "Well, what?

"'Basile, go to her! Ah! how terrible it is!' said she.

"'Go to her?' I asked myself; and immediately I made answer to myself that I ought to go, that probably that was the thing that is usually done when a husband like myself kills his wife, that it was absolutely necessary that I should go and see her.

"'If that is the proper thing, I must go,' I repeated to myself. 'Yes, if it is necessary, I shall still have time,' said I to myself, thinking of my intent of blowing my brains out.

"And I followed my sister-in-law.

"'Now there are going to be words and faces, but I will not yield,' I declared to myself.

"'Wait,' said I to my sister-in-law, 'it is not right to be without shoes. Let me put something on my feet.'"

Chapter XXVIII

"Strange thing! Again, when I had left my study, and was passing through the familiar rooms, again the hope came to me that nothing had happened. But the odor of the drugs being applied brought me back to a sense of reality.

"'No, everything has happened.'

"In passing through the hall, beside the children's room, I saw little Lise. She was looking at me with eyes full of fear. I even thought that all the children were looking at me.

"As I approached the door of our sleeping-room, one of the help opened it from within, and came out.

"The first thing that I noticed when I entered was HER light gray dress upon a chair, all dark with blood. On our common bed she was stretched, with knees drawn up.

"She lay very high, upon pillows, her slip half open. A cloth had been placed on the wound. A heavy smell of drugs filled the room. More than anything else, I was shocked at her face, which was swollen and black under the eyes and over a part of the nose.

"This was the result of the blow that I had struck her with my elbow, when she had tried to hold me back. Of beauty there was no trace left. I saw something ugly in her.

"I stopped in the door-way.

"'Approach, approach her,' said her sister.

"'Yes, probably she is sorry,' thought I. 'Shall I forgive her? Yes, she is dying, I must forgive her,' I added..

"I approached the bedside.

"With difficulty she raised her eyes, one of which was swollen, and uttered these words with difficulty: 'You have accomplished what you desired. You have killed me.'

"And in her face, through the physical sufferings, in the approach of death, was expressed the same old hate so familiar to me.

"'The children . . . I will not give them to you . . . all the same. . . . She (her sister) shall take them.' . . .

"But of that which I considered essential, of her fault, of her treason, one would have said that she did not think it necessary to say even a word.

"'Yes, take joy in what you have done.'

"And she wept.

"At the door stood her sister with the children.

"'Yes, see what you have done!'

"I cast a glance at the children, and then at her black and swollen face, and for the first time I forgot myself (my rights, my pride), and for the first time I saw in her a human being, a sister.

"And all that which a moment before had been so terrible to me now seemed of little importance – all this lack of trust. Now the opposite was true.

"What I had done seemed to me so important that I felt like bending over, putting my face to her hand, and saying: 'Forgive me!'

"But I did not dare. She was silent, her eyes lowered, evidently having no strength to speak further. Then the face I had made black with my elbow began to tremble and grow small. She weakly pushed me back.

"'Why has all this happened? Why?'

"'Forgive me,' said I.

"'Yes, if you had not killed me,' she cried suddenly, and her eyes shone with fever. 'Forgiving – that is nothing. . . . If I only do not die! Ah, you have accomplished what you desired! I hate you!'

"Then she became out of her mind. She was fearful, and cried: "'Fire, I do not fear . . . but strike them all . . . He has gone. . . . He has gone.' . . .

"The craziness continued. She no longer recognized the children, not even little Lise, who had approached.

"Toward noon she died.

"As for me, I was arrested before her death, at eight o'clock in the morning. They took me to the police station, then to prison, and there, during the eleven months I waited for the court's decision, I thought about myself, and my past, and I understood it. Yes, I began to understand from the third day, when they took me to the house."

Posdnicheff seemed to wish to add something, but, no longer having the strength to hold back his tears, he stopped. After a few minutes, recovering his calmness, he went on:

"I began to understand only when I saw her dead body." He uttered a cry, and then immediately continued: "Then only, when I saw her dead face, did I understand all that I had done. I understood that it was I, I, who had killed her.

"I understood that I was the cause of the fact that she, who had been a moving, living, breathing being, had now become still and cold, and that there was no way of repairing this thing. He who has not lived through that cannot understand it."

He was silent a long time. Posdnicheff wept and trembled before me. His face had become delicate and long, and his mouth had grown larger.

"Yes," said he suddenly, "if I had known what I now know, I should never have married her, never, not for anything."

Again we remained silent for a long time.

"Yes, that is what I have done, that is my experience, We must understand the real meaning of the words of the Gospel, Matthew, V. 28, 'that whoever looks on a woman to desire her has sinned'. These words relate to the wife, to the sister, and not only to the wife of another, but especially to one's own wife."

THE END

JOSEPH COWLEY, born on October 9, 1923, graduated from Columbia University in 1947. He interrupted his academic career to serve two and a half years with the Army Air Force during World War II. The last months of service were spent overseas as a bombardier with the Eighth Air Force, for which he was awarded the Bronze Star.

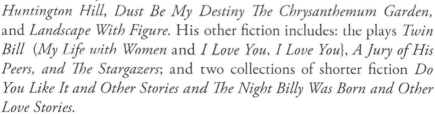

He received his M.A. from Columbia in 1948 and taught English at Cornell before entering sales. His career was spent writing and editing material on sales and management for The Research Institute of America, before taking early retirement in 1982 to work on his fiction and other books.

Joseph Cowley is the author of the novels *Home by Seven*, *The House on Huntington Hill*, *Dust Be My Destiny The Chrysanthemum Garden*, and *Landscape With Figure*. His other fiction includes: the plays *Twin Bill* (*My Life with Women* and *I Love You, I Love You*}, *A Jury of His Peers, and The Stargazers*; and two collections of shorter fiction *Do You Like It and Other Stories and The Night Billy Was Born and Other Love Stories*.

He has authored two books of non-fiction: *John Adams: Architect of Freedom,* and *The Executive Strategist, An Armchair Guide to Scientific Decision-Making.* (with Robert Weisselberg)

He recently adapted *Crime and Punishment* by Dostoevsky and *The Scarlet Letter* by Hawthorne for ESL students and the general reader. *The Kreutzer Sonata* by Tolstoy is the third volume in this series called *Classics Condensed by Cowley.*

His articles have appeared in trade and science journals like *Our Army* and *Mechanix Illustrated*, and his short stories in *The Maryland Review, Prairie Schooner, New-Story, Ohio Short Fiction*, and other literary journals and anthologies.

Joseph Cowley is listed in a number of reference volumes, among them: Who's Who, *International Who's Who of Writers and Authors, Who's Who in the World, Strathmore's Who's Who, The Cambridge Blue Book,* and *2000 Outstanding Intellectuals of the 21st Century.*

Among the organizations he has been associated with are Mensa, the Authors Guild, and the *Great Books Program*, where he led discussions and served on the L.I. Council for Great Books.